MAYHEM AND EMBER

FIRE WITCHES OF SALEM
BOOK FOUR

CARRIE PULKINEN

CHAPTER I
EMBER

Six months ago, if you'd told me I'd get a haircut from an imp, I'd have called you crazy. If you would've said I'd lose my sword in a twenty-foot-deep crevice beneath the biggest church in town, I'd have laughed. And the mere mention that my baby sister would be getting it on with a demon prince in the room down the hall would've had me in stitches.

Yet here we were...and the haircut wasn't even a good one.

I rummaged through my mom's sewing kit and grabbed her sharpest pair of fabric scissors before returning it to the shelf and padding across the living room in my socks. My door was the first on the left. Beyond that, Patrice slept in Cinder's bed, and at the end of the hall, Miles and Shade shared my parents' space. In between, Ash lay in her bedroom, snuggled up with Chaos, Prince of Hell.

I shook my head. That wasn't even the craziest thing that had happened over the past few weeks.

After flipping on the light, I strode through my room and stepped into the bathroom. I could hardly bear my reflection. I'd showered and even put on a bit of makeup this morning, so I didn't look terrible—aside from my hair—but the tightness of my eyes and the set of my jaw told the story of a woman who'd had the crushing weight of the entire world thrust onto her back in one fell swoop.

And she wasn't sure how much longer she could carry it.

"One thing at a time, Em," I said to the woman I barely recognized. "Focus on the things you can control. Complete one task, and then you can worry about the next." Otherwise, I might curl into a ball on the floor and cease to exist.

Up first, fixing my hideous hair.

I glared at the side the imp had chopped off with a pair of garden shears. Granted, the slimy little sucker was going for my neck, so I should've been glad he only took off ten inches of hair. But it would take me at least two years to grow it back to the length I liked.

Switching my focus to the long purple locks on the other side of my head, I sighed. This was a thing I could control. A problem I could solve, even if the solution wasn't appealing in the slightest.

I gathered a fistful in my hand and closed the scissors around it. I tried to, at least, but my hair was too thick. Working the blades open and closed, I sawed off a clump, leaving jagged edges and lament in its wake.

"Oh, honey. Let me help you." Ash's voice startled me, and I jumped, dropping the scissors into the sink.

"I didn't hear you come in." I picked them up and grabbed another fistful of hair.

"Give them to me." She held out her hand, so I placed the handles in her palm. "That little bugger did a number on you, didn't he?" She grabbed some clips and pinned up the top layer of my hair.

"It's driving me bonkers. One side is too short to pull back, and the other gets in my way if I don't." I rested my hands on the edge of the sink and focused on the coolness of the porcelain seeping into my skin and the scent of citrus emanating from the plug-in air freshener next to the mirror. "Where's your demon?"

"In the shower." She began snipping, ten-inch-long strands of purple falling around my feet. "What's our next move?"

I ground my teeth even harder. "I want my sword."

She paused, pursing her lips before continuing my haircut. "You don't need it to fight. You could stop a monster with a spell and your bare hands if you had to."

"I want it," I said, my bottom teeth never losing contact with my top. "It's as much a part of me as my hideous hair."

"It won't be hideous much longer." She unpinned a section and snipped some more. "I'm sure the church is closed. The foundation can't support it after what Mayhem and Chrys did to it, and I doubt they'll let us in."

I lowered my gaze at the mention of our once-friend, Chrys. Her body still lay under enchantment in our basement. Hopefully, her mother would claim it soon.

Snapping my eyes to the mirror, I looked at my sister. "So what if it's closed? That's never stopped us before."

"You could get a new one." She cut the last section and began evening it out.

I turned my head to see her. "Why would I do that when I can retrieve my old one?"

With her fingers on my scalp, she turned me toward the mirror. "We still have to summon Mayhem, find Cinder and then our parents, all the while battling the bigger and badder beasties that are slipping through the veil. The less conflict we put upon ourselves the better." She shrugged. "It would be easier to get a new one."

"There's a six-month waiting list to have one forged, and anyway..." I picked up a piece of hair from the sink and slid my fingers over the smooth strands. "Mom gave it to me for my twenty-second birthday. It's special."

Ash's expression softened. "I hear you. All right. Step one: retrieve your sword. Step two: re-summon Mayhem the right way. Step three: break the curse and save the world."

"You make it sound so simple." I dropped the hair and returned my hands to the edge of the sink.

"We both know it's not." She ran her fingers through my locks, shaking them out. "There you go. I think the length suits you."

I turned my head from side to side, examining her work. Slightly longer than chin length, my hair felt lighter and looked thicker and healthier. "Not bad, sis. Is there anything you aren't good at?"

She laughed and said, "Be right back," before slipping out of the bathroom and returning with a broom and dustpan.

As we cleaned up the hair and dropped it into the trash can, I eyed the demonic sigil on my sister's arm. The thing that linked her to Chaos. She swore she was in love with the demon, but I had to wonder if the magical tattoo she'd given herself wasn't responsible for fabricating the emotions.

"Aren't you going to remove that?" I followed her out of the room and into the kitchen.

"Chaos says it's safer if I keep it. Mayhem is royally

pissed, and as long as I bear Chaos's mark, he won't hurt me." She filled the coffee machine with grounds.

"Is that what he says?" I crossed my arms, unconvinced. Demons were liars, or so I'd been taught. I'd actually never had a conversation with one until Chaos came into our lives, but I had a feeling his brother was as pissed at him as he was at us. A tattoo wouldn't keep anyone safe, no matter how much vim she'd put into it.

Ash sighed and turned to face me. "I know it's hard to comprehend, but I promise you... Whether I have this tattoo or not, I am in love with Chaos and he loves me. I'm not asking you to understand it, but I do need you to accept it."

It made no sense, a light witch and a demon from the Underworld fitting so well together, but they did. While I hated to admit it, they seemed almost perfect for each other...in an opposites-attract, forbidden-love kind of way.

Oh, for Hecate's sake. I didn't even read romance novels, but Ash had talked so much about them and her favorite tropes, I felt like I'd read dozens. "You're right. What do I know about love?"

As if on cue, the demon emerged from the hallway and strode across the room to sweep Ash into his arms. "Good morning, little witch."

He planted a kiss on her lips, and her energy

shifted, exuding calmness. Pulling away, he winked at her before turning to me. "Ember," he said with a nod.

I didn't have to understand, only accept. "Where's Mayhem's skull?"

"In a drawer in Ash's room, where it will stay until we're ready to summon him." He opened the pantry and pulled out three boxes of cereal.

"I put a ward on it." Ash took six mugs from the cabinet. "Just in case."

"Good." I set a gallon of milk on the counter next to the bowls Ash had lined up.

"When you summon my brother, I suggest you combine the power of all five witches to create the containment circle." Chaos poured a bowl of the sugariest cereal we had, cramming a handful into his mouth before adding the milk. "He's a force when he isn't angry. I'm afraid he'll be a hurricane after what we've done."

I shook my head. "You're talking a step ahead. We have to focus on one thing at a time."

"And first on the to-do list is returning to the church to get her sword." Ash poured three cups of coffee and handed them to us before sinking onto a stool at the counter.

"Can't you get a new sword?" Shade strode into the kitchen and poured himself a bowl of Raisin Bran. "I replace my knives all the time."

My teeth clicked. How I despised redundant conversations.

"It was a gift from our mother," Ash answered for me. "And there's a six-month waiting list for forging enchanted silver."

"Is it safe to go down there?" Patrice emerged from the hallway, followed by Miles. "The building shook and groaned against the crevices. It might not even be standing this morning."

"All the more reason to get this done now. Eat up." I popped a protein bar into my mouth, put on my boots, and headed downstairs to the storage room, grimacing as I passed Chrys's body. We had cleaned her up and laid her on a table before casting a preservation spell and covering her with a sheet. That had been difficult enough. Calling her mother with the news, well... Ash had volunteered for that job, and I'd been happy to hand over the reins.

I let my gaze wander over her outline beneath the sheet, my chest tightening with emotions I couldn't name. I still couldn't comprehend the betrayal. Her last words were *I had no choice*. But there was always a choice, and hers was obvious. Why she chose the dark side, I had no idea. Nothing about what happened with her made sense.

But I couldn't think about that now. I had a coven to run, a world to save, and no clue how to do either.

Thirty feet of enchanted nylon rope hung on the

wall next to a shelving unit filled with supplies for our shop. We hadn't been open to the public in weeks. We relied on the income to pay the taxes and utilities for the building, but at the rate we were going, we'd be sitting in the dark before long. I hadn't been to work in weeks either. Honestly, I was surprised they hadn't fired me yet.

I grabbed the magically strengthened rope, slung it over my shoulder, and did my best to ignore the body in the basement as I made my way upstairs.

Chaos and Ash stood at the sink, washing dishes, which was weird as all get-out. My little sister had domesticated a demon. Go figure.

My phone chimed as I lay the rope on the counter, and I fished it out of my pocket to find a message from Chief Higgins. "Well, shit."

"What?" Miles asked.

I rolled my neck, stretching out the tension. "Another rift opened last night inside the monster museum. Chief called them oversized mosquitoes, so I assume it's a swarm of fae."

"We can take care of it," Miles said. "Go get your sword, and we'll rendezvous here in an hour."

A sinking sensation formed in my gut, but I pursed my lips and ignored it. I hated splitting up the team— strength in numbers and all—but we were running out of time. "Do we have any bottled shadow spells left?"

Ash grabbed her bag from a hook on the wall and peered inside. "Three."

"Give them to Miles." I turned to him. "Can you and Patrice handle it? I don't know how long this will take, so I need Shade with me to keep us cloaked."

He cut his gaze to his friend before nodding. "We've got this, right, Patrice?"

"Freeze them, shove them through, and seal the rift. Easy-peasy." She took the bottled mending spell Ash offered.

"Good." I slung the rope over my shoulder. "Let's head out."

Shade rode shotgun while Ash and Chaos took the back seat in the van, and we made our way to the scene of the crime. Thankfully, the drive was an uneventful one. No dark witch minions tried to stop us this time, though I wouldn't have minded a little scuffle. Fighting I was good at. Hecate knew I sucked at being High Priestess.

"We need to be on alert for Boston witches." I rolled to a stop two blocks from the church and killed the engine.

"You don't think they ran off to lick their wounds?" Shade adjusted the straps of his knife harness. "Without their leader, they're probably trying to act like nothing happened so they don't get banished."

"Or they could be organizing again." Ash looped

her satchel over her head to wear it cross-body. "Who knows how dark witches think?"

"Either way, be on high alert. Cloak us, Shade." I waited for our shadow witch to do his thing. Once the fog rolled around us, turning the outside world grayscale, I hopped out of the van and opened the side door before lifting the hatch out of habit.

My shoulders slumped at the empty space where my sword should have lain. The daggers strapped to my thighs and ankles would have to do if we ran into trouble. And honestly...I hoped we would. Fighting was in my blood. Being locked in battle was the one time I could clear my head, shut off my thoughts, and let my instincts take over. Whatever daunting task that lay six steps ahead didn't matter in that moment. All I had to do was kick butt, no name-taking required.

"We'll get it back." Ash rested a hand on my back, and I straightened, grabbing an extra knife to hide my emotional display.

The coven thinking I was a weak crybaby was the last thing I needed. I shut the door and turned to Chaos, who carried the rope. "That's not fireproof, so put it down if you're going to light yourself ablaze."

He raised his brows. "Are you expecting a battle?"

"I'm always ready for a fight." I jerked my head toward the church, and, invisible to the rest of the world, we strode two blocks toward the entrance.

Caution tape looped through a makeshift chain-link fence surrounded the property, and a stout man in a hardhat held an iPad toward a woman in a tailored suit. I raised my hand, telling my team to stop and listen to their conversation.

"I don't know how an earthquake could have only affected this small area," the man said. "Are you sure it wasn't an act of God? Is the congregation worshipping false idols or something?" He guffawed at his own bad joke.

The woman flashed an indignant look and crossed her arms. "Can the foundation be repaired?"

"It'll cost a pretty penny, but we can do it." He swiped his finger on the iPad, and I motioned for the others to follow.

Ash hurried to walk beside me. "At least they can fix it. I wonder how they'll get the money though."

"I'm sure the congregation will pay for it." I stopped beside a piece of fence that wasn't fastened to the next section and moved it forward, creating enough space for us to pass through.

My mood darkened as we approached the entrance, and when I grabbed the door handle, Ash let out a muffled sound of disapproval. I hadn't let her check for magic before I touched it.

I motioned to the door. "Humans are in control here. Nobody put up a ward on a church that could collapse at any minute. It is locked, though."

"We still have to use caution. Confess, expose,

my magic sleuth. I call on you to reveal your truth." She cast her magic-revealing spell, finding nothing, as I expected, before tugging a lock-picking kit from her satchel and going to work. "Better safe than sorry."

"Sometimes, too careful can get you killed," I said.

"There's no such thing as too careful these days." She smiled triumphantly and opened the door.

I strode inside, heading straight to the passage that led to the underground. The building groaned as we made our way through the dark, twisting halls and descended stair after stair. Scents of decay and dust clung to the air particles, making my nostrils feel like sandpaper with each inhale, and a humming sound vibrated through the basement as we approached the entrance to the room where it all went down. I stopped, turning and giving my team a questioning look.

"I sense a rift." Chaos rested a hand on Ash's lower back and closed his eyes. "Lower-level demons and something...other."

Shade took two knives from his harness, gripping them tightly. "Of course this couldn't be easy."

"Where's the fun in easy?" I nodded to Ash's bag. "Get the freezing and mending spells ready. Chaos, you handle the demons. The rest of us will take care of the 'other.'"

Without a word, he brushed past me and entered

the room. I followed on his heels, and Ash and Shade took up the rear of our hunting crew.

Inside, we found total chaos, and I don't mean my sister's boyfriend.

A swarm of lesser fae, with their brown wings and razor teeth, swooped this way and that, dive-bombing a group of imps. Hadn't we dealt with these little shits enough?

The imps fought back, throwing books, religious artifacts, scraps of wood...anything they could get their slimy little hands on, and I cracked my knuckles. I hated imps more than I hated fae.

Chaos shouted, "Stop," and even though the fae kept attacking, the imps obeyed the Prince of Hell's command and skittered toward him like good little puppies.

"Standing tall or on your knees, in the name of the goddess, I force you to freeze," Ash cast the spell, and the oversized mosquitoes stopped midair.

My chest swelled with pride. My little sis had grown so much over the past few weeks, finally coming into her power. Power strong enough to take out the entire coven if the curse came to fruition...

I could not let that happen.

Chaos ordered the imps through the rift before helping Ash and Shade shove the fae through. I paced to the massive crevice Chrys and Mayhem had opened in an attempt to kill us and peered over the edge.

Darkness engulfed the bottom of the pit, but my sword lay down there somewhere. I grabbed the rope Chaos had dropped and looped it around one thigh and then the other, making a harness so they could lower me.

A sinister growl that sounded more alien than animal reverberated in the shadows to my right. I swiveled my head toward it, and out stepped one of the ugliest creatures I'd ever seen.

CHAPTER 2

EMBER

He stood five and a half feet tall, with stark white—was it hair or fur?—atop his almost-human head. Two insect-like antennae jutted up from his scalp, bending forward like an ant, and enormous black eyes locked onto me as his thin lips—for lack of a better word—peeled back to reveal pointy, dagger-like teeth.

He took a step toward me, and his massive, brown cockroach wings fluttered, the sound reminding me of the nasty insects that dive-bombed me when I visited Texas one summer. A shiver spiraled down my spine before lurching into my stomach and making it turn.

What was it about humidity and bugs? Ick.

I grabbed a dagger from my thigh holster and widened my stance. "Chaos, are you going to take care of this guy or do I get to vanquish him?" I snapped my head toward my team and found Ash sealing the rift.

"Wait! We missed one." But I was too late. The fabric of reality stitched together before my eyes, and I jerked my gaze back to the beastie in question.

The giant roach-man sprung, half-running, half-flying toward me and screaming like a swarm of cicadas. I swung a dagger, hitting a wing, and let me tell you, those friggin' things were like armor. The moment the blade made impact, it snapped, the force reverberating up my arm and into my jaw, making my teeth ache.

He lashed out a clawed hand and ripped my shirt. I jabbed the knife at his chest, but the second blade broke as easily as the first. What the hell was this thing made of? Titanium?

With an ear-splitting screech, he slammed into me, grasping my shoulders in his claws and tackling me. My back smacked the ground, and all the air left my lungs in a *whoosh*. I gasped, which was a huge mistake. Roachman sneered, and a glob of gooey saliva landed right in my mouth.

It tasted like salty snot and regret.

I spit it back at him and gagged as I struggled beneath his weight. Someone...it could have been Ash or Chaos...threw a fireball at him, and it bounced off his roach armor, not singeing it a bit.

He growled, and another bit of gooey mess hung

from the corner of his lip, threatening to hit my face. I kept my mouth closed this time and grabbed a dagger from my holster. What good it would do, I had no clue, but I refused to become breakfast for a cockroach.

He reared his head back, ready to chomp my face, and I caught a glimpse of a chink in his armor. I jabbed the dagger into the soft spot just below his ear hole, and praise the goddess, it didn't break. Roachman squealed and rolled off me, and I scrambled to my feet.

Ash threw the binding spell at him, but he flapped his blade-proof wings and jetted to the ceiling before it reached him, hanging on like he had suction cups in his hands and feet.

"What the hell, Chaos?" I hocked up the biggest loogie I could and spit the rest of the roach goo from my mouth. "Make your demon friend behave."

"He's not a demon." Ash grabbed my arm and dragged me out from under the creature from not-Hell. "He's a fae."

"What?" I fumbled with the rope still tied around me like a harness. "How did he get so big?"

"He's midlevel," Chaos said. "Most likely a scout for the greater fae horde."

"Fabulous." I got one knot untied when the flitting of roach wings assaulted the air and the sucker swooped to the ground, grabbing the rope that was still tied to one leg and jutting upward to the ceiling once more.

My feet left the floor with a jerk of his arm, and he hauled me halfway up, leaving me dangling upside down like a witchy chandelier in the middle of the room.

Blood rushed to my head, but I swung myself upright and grabbed the rope. "How do I kill him?"

"Beheading is the fastest way," Chaos said. "Unless you can find an opening in his exoskeleton to stab his heart."

I freed my other leg from the harness and glared up at Roachman. He yanked my dagger from his neck and hurled it to the ground, heaving a giant breath against the pain. As his chest expanded, so did his armor, revealing an opening right beneath his heart. Or...where I assumed his heart would be.

Lifting my leg, I snatched a knife from my ankle holster and silently prayed to the goddess it would be long enough to reach the prize. Clutching the metal handle between my teeth, I hauled myself up the rope, which was a lot harder than I remembered from gym class. When all this was over, I needed to hit the weights.

I peered down at Ash, who rummaged through her spell kit, no doubt trying to concoct something to weaken his armor. Chaos kneeled beside her, taking the ingredient bottles as she handed them to him, and Shade...

Was he on his phone?

"Bastard," I mumbled around the steel between my teeth. Returning my attention to Roachman, I hauled myself up a little farther, but my vision wavered and my lips suddenly didn't feel the coolness of the handle pressed against them. My whole mouth went numb.

Nausea churned in my gut, and I gagged. The knife fell to the ground, and I tried to move my jaw, to speak, to scream, to...anything.

But I couldn't feel my face.

"Don't let him bite you, Ember," Shade called and held up his phone. "According to the witchy web, these guys are venomous."

Fan-friggin'-tastic. That explained the numbness spreading down my neck.

I hurried a few feet down the rope and let go. My knees buckled when I hit the ground, and I rolled before jutting to my feet again.

"Heh..." was the only sound I could muster, so I pointed to my mouth and pressed my hands against my cheeks and my head.

Ash's face pinched with concern. "He already got you?"

I nodded.

"If you can bring him down, I've got a softening spell that might weaken him enough to get a knife through." She held up a steaming copper bowl.

If I'd had my sword, I would've lobbed his head clean off by now.

"Hey, ugly." Shade hurled a knife, but it bounced off Roachman's armor and tumbled into the crevice where my sword lay, out of reach. He tried again, this time hitting an impenetrable wing.

If my mouth worked, I could have told them about the two soft spots I'd found, but my tongue had swollen to the size of a lemon. I couldn't close my lips, much less make sound pass from them. Hell, it was a miracle I could even breathe.

"Are you sure that spell won't reach the ceiling?" Shade asked. "Or what about hellfire?"

Chaos flexed his fingers, gathering fire in his palms before shooting it toward our foe. The Roachman screeched and wrapped his wings around his body, shielding himself from the flames. As the demon called his fire back, smoke billowed from the creature's form.

Cracks spread across his rigid wings, the surface peeling from the heat of Hell, but Roachman hung on, hissing and fluttering, raining charred bits of wing onto us.

"You'll have to go hotter." Ash poured the powdered potion into her hand and closed her fingers around it.

"I hit it with everything I have. I will try again." He gathered more hellfire, and I turned to the mess the imps had made of the basement. Surely there was something here I could throw at the beastie. My last knife attached to my ankle had a blade only three inches long. Even if I could get it beneath the armor, it wouldn't pierce the heart.

While Chaos worked on barbecued roach fae, Ash and Shade whipped up another potion. I threw boards aside, rummaging through artifacts and tools the church stored in their basement. Sadly, no razor-sharp swords lay in the clutter, but a pair of hatchets caught my eye.

I stumbled over a prayer bench, twisting my ankle as I stepped on the edge of a two-by-four. The numbness from the fae venom spread into my shoulders and down my chest, squeezing my heart and lungs until it felt like I was breathing through a straw.

I managed to grab the hatchets, but as I rose, I tipped backward, crashing into the shelving unit attached to the wall. My vision tunneled, my pulse slowing until I could barely stay conscious.

"Hold on, Em!" Ash kneeled next to me, her blue hair barely registering in my pin-prick-sized field of vision. She poured a potion into my mouth. At least, I assumed that was what she did. I'd lost feeling everywhere except my legs.

"Here's the second one." Shade handed something to her, and my vision dimmed into darkness, my breaths slowing, ceasing.

A tickle formed in my throat, spreading into my

chest and down my arms. I gasped, and the breath I raked in filled my lungs fully, making them burn. My lids flew open, my blurry vision swimming back into focus, and I sat upright, gasping again before coughing like a teenager the first time they took a hit of a blunt.

"He has...soft spots," I said between coughs.

They helped me to my feet, and we crawled over the mess to stand next to Chaos. He breathed heavily, sweat beading on his brow as he blasted another heat-wave at the fae.

"That's enough." Ash clutched his arm. "You might be immortal, but you can still get vanquished. Save your strength. Ember has a plan."

I peered up at Roachman clinging to the ceiling. His back faced us, but his charred wings had retracted, leaving his head exposed.

"His exoskeleton lies in layers over his chest, like fish scales," I said. "We can stab him beneath one if you've got a long enough knife."

"If we can get him down." Shade held up a weapon. "It's my last one."

Clutching the hatchets in one hand, I retrieved my three-inch knife and traded him for the long one. "He's also soft beneath his ear holes. Aim for that, and make it count."

He nodded once and threw the blade. It rotated through the air and hit home, right in the fae's neck.

The beastie let out a pained screech, losing his grip on the ceiling and hanging on by one clawed hand.

I hurled the first hatchet at his wrist, but he swung, shielding himself with a burned wing. He reached his other hand to the ceiling, and I threw, the hatchet tumbling head over handle and slicing into my target.

Roachman fell, his amputated claw still clinging to the ceiling as his back smacked the ground. Ash hit him with a freezing spell, and I stood over him, a nine-inch dagger clutched in my hand.

"Don't *ever* try to come between a woman and her sword." Lifting an armor plate, I jabbed the dagger into his flesh and twisted before yanking it out and thrusting it in again. "And never try to swap spit without consent."

The fae raked in a breath and wheezed, "Our... world...now." His head lolled to the side, and he stilled, his lifeforce returning to the ether.

"Since when can fae talk?" I wiped my hands on my pants and straightened.

"His level and higher always could." Chaos jostled the corpse with his boot. It didn't move.

"In English?" I picked up the rope and made another harness, wrapping it around my thighs and tying it at my waist.

"They learn quickly, as do demons." He helped Ash

return the supplies to her bag. "Did you think English was my first language?"

"I never gave it much thought. Here…" I tossed the end of the rope toward him. "Make use of your brute strength and lower me into the pit. I want my sword, and then I want a scorching hot shower. I hate roaches almost as much as I hate rats."

He gripped the rope and slowly lowered me into the crevice. With my feet against the dirt wall, I rappelled twenty feet and hit bottom. "Don't let go," I shouted and turned on my phone's flashlight.

The hole was massive, somehow growing wider at the bottom than it was at the top, and I had to wonder how much of this was Chrys's doing versus Mayhem's. Chrys was a powerful witch; she'd shown us that plenty of times before she summoned the demon into her head.

But was she this strong? Sadly, we would never know.

I shined the light around the dirt and caught a glimmer of enchanted silver. "There's my baby."

I grabbed her handle and swung her in two perfectly balanced figure eights before gripping her with both hands and sending fire licking up the blade. *Ahhh…That's more like it.*

After extinguishing the flames, I holstered the sword in my back scabbard, picked up Shade's dagger, and shouted, "Bring me up."

Chaos pulled me out of the crevice, and I untied the rope, freeing myself from the harness. I shot a flame at the fae's body, trying to cremate the beastie, but his armor protected him from the fire, even in death. I barely singed him. "It's like these suckers were made to be a fire witch's sworn enemy."

"All three of us together?' Ash asked.

"It's worth a shot." I sent out another flame, giving it all the heat I had, and Chaos and my sister did the same. The exoskeleton burned a bit, flaking like the wings had done when Chaos hit them earlier, but it would take us an hour to turn the giant cockroach to ash.

Sweat beaded on my forehead, and my breaths became labored. Fire was my inborn gift, so it didn't tax my vim, but this much exertion took a physical toll on my body.

And that pissed me off royally.

"Burn you overgrown insect." My anger sparked more flames inside me, and I pushed out another heatwave. Dead or alive, this sucker would not get the best of me.

"You're wearing yourselves out," Shade said. "And I can't keep us cloaked forever. Let's push him into the crevice and be done."

"Works for me." Ash extinguished her fire like she'd had control of it her entire life, and Chaos followed suit.

My nostrils flared on an irritated exhale, but he was right. We had too much shit to do to waste our energy on a dead fae. "All right, but I get the honors."

I stomped toward the roach and rolled him to the crevice. With my boot against his shoulder, I shoved him over the edge. He hit the ground with a satisfying *thud*, and I wiped my hands on my jeans.

"Let's go summon a demon prince." The words barely had time to cross my lips before my phone buzzed. I swiped open the screen and groaned. "There's *another* rift."

CHAPTER 3
MAYHEM

All I saw was darkness. All I heard was silence. All I felt was pure primal rage.

I was finally free of my prison, my spirit possessing a witch of such immense power I could move earth, making it swallow my enemies whole. Burning through her body and claiming it as my own would have allowed me to keep her magic, adding it to mine and becoming more powerful than Chaos and Discord combined. I could have rivaled Lucifer himself.

But the blue-haired witch...the one they called Ash...ruined it all. My host's body was no match for the binding spells she'd cast on us. If my vessel had given up control when I demanded it, I could have broken free. But my insolent human receptacle had refused.

She was a witch after all, and witches were the

vilest creatures to ever walk the earth. I would be freed from this dark prison sooner or later, and when I was, I would find a way to their side of the veil and kill them all for what they'd done.

And my brother...

I imagined my hands curling into fists at the thought of the traitorous bastard, my talons digging into my wrists, the phantom pain the only thing reminding me I still existed in this realm of sensory deprivation.

Chaos would pay for his betrayal. Whether he'd willingly gone along with their subterfuge or he'd been bound under a spell didn't matter. I would take revenge, and I would start by killing the one he claimed to love.

CHAPTER 4
EMBER

"It's a good thing the rift happened in a witch's backyard." Ash set black candles around the circle of salt she'd poured while I eyed the skull.

It looked like a regular human, yet the energy it exuded felt like pinpricks running through my muscles when I touched it. "Right? Monkeys can only escape from the zoo so many times before the humans get suspicious."

Police Chief Higgins, one of the few mundane in Salem who knew real magic existed, had explained away an imp attack in a hardware store by calling them monkeys. Today, a trio of the buggers had made it through a tiny rift in Inga's yard, and thankfully, she'd messaged me before getting anyone else involved.

Dragging my gaze away from Mayhem's severed head, I admired the near-perfect ring Ash had poured. We'd decided to perform the summoning in her studio, away from the windows of the storefront—and the prying eyes of passersby—and far from the irreplaceable grimoires in the library.

Her tattoo equipment sat on a counter against the wall, and a wooden storage unit stood in the corner. LED track lighting hung from the ceiling, casting the room in artificial brightness, but we'd be dimming those soon. Magic worked better in candlelight...especially for fire witches.

Clutching the salt in both hands, my sister bounced her gaze from the floor to me three times before she finally held eye contact. "At the rate the veil is thinning, we'll need to bring in more of the coven to help keep the beasties at bay. You know that, right?"

I clenched my jaw. She was right. I knew she was, but it didn't make it any easier to admit. "If we tell them everything..." I blew out a hard breath. "They're going to blame me. I'm responsible for this coven, and everything is going to shit."

"No one will blame you."

Yes, they would, and they should. "If Mom and Cinder were here, they'd know exactly what to do. They don't make mistakes like I do."

Ash gave me a WTF look, lifting one hand and dropping it at her side. "All of this is happening *because* of Mom and Cinder's mistakes. Mom messed with the wrong demon. Cinder acted alone when we could have helped her. They screwed up too."

I fought to keep my lower lip from pouting. Why did my little sister always make such good points?

"And we won't have to tell them everything." She shook her head, drumming her fingers on the canister. "It's almost Halloween, so some thinning is natural. We'll say the rest is Chrys's fault. That she summoned a demon to take over the coven, but you stopped her."

I laughed dryly. "You mean *you* stopped her. You performed the exorcism and the vanquishing."

"Which I couldn't have done without you. I don't need any of the credit." She caught her bottom lip between her teeth. "You might have to stop me soon if we can't get to Cinder and Discord before I…"

"Hey. Stop that." I clutched her shoulders, dipping my head to catch her gaze. "We're going to break the curse."

"Or die trying." She smiled sadly and shrugged out of my grasp. "I don't know, Em. Some of the thoughts I have aren't very light-witch-like. Here." She handed me the salt and tugged her phone from her pocket.

I looked at the canister, the little girl with her umbrella and yellow dress taunting me, and put it next to the skull. These witches were my responsibility. Mom and Cinder might have started the trouble, but *I* was to blame for the ones who had died. "We won't lose anyone else."

"Not if we can help it." She handed the phone to me and offered a piece of chalk. "Draw Mayhem's sigil in the center of the circle, and we'll be ready to activate the containment when the others get back."

"Me?" I held the phone and chalk toward her. "You're the artist. This is your wheelhouse."

She raised her hands, refusing to accept them. "It doesn't feel right for me to do it. He's not my demon."

"Well, he's not mine either. I'd rather not have anything to do with him." I set the items next to the skull and crossed my arms. "And you better get whatever romance novel trope you're thinking of out of your head. Just because you like getting it on with a demon doesn't mean I want to."

She laughed. "I'm not trying to set you up with Chaos's brother, but one Prince of Hell is all I can handle. Mayhem will owe whoever draws his sigil a favor, and I would rather it not be me."

"But you're good at handling demons."

"I'm good with *my* demon. It's someone else's turn, and that someone is you."

I glared at Ash and picked up the chalk. "Fine. But don't even think about putting his mark anywhere on my skin. The faster we break the curse and send the demons back to hell, the better."

A shadow crossed her features, her gaze drifting to

the floor as she drew her shoulders upward. She straightened, looking at me as if my third eye were suddenly visible, and shook her head. "Do you even hear yourself when you speak?"

"What kind of a question is that?" I squinted at the sigil on the phone and kneeled at the edge of the ring.

"Guess not." She bumped her fist onto the salt canister, closing the little metal spout. "Tell me what you said."

I sighed and sat back on my heels, searching my brain for whatever wrong thing I might have uttered. "I told you I don't want his mark on my skin."

She crossed her arms. "After that."

The tension in my neck increased, causing an ache at the base of my skull. You'd think, after unlocking her full power and getting her brains banged out nightly by the supposed love of her life, she'd be less emotional... Oh.

Well, feck. "I'm sorry, Ash. I didn't mean—"

"You didn't mean the sooner I lost my soulmate the better?"

"No, I didn't." I glanced at the sigil again and pressed the chalk to the wooden floor, dragging it downward before looping back up. "I wasn't thinking about that part of our predicament."

"You never do," she mumbled under her breath.

I pretended not to hear. Goddess knew I wasn't the best when it came to peopling. Tiptoeing around emotions and sugar-coating words had never been my strong suit; that was no secret. It wasn't often I thought to ask a ghoul how its day was before lobbing off its head.

"It goes left." Ash squatted next to me and pointed at the design.

I compared what I'd drawn to the image on the screen. "Damn, you're right. Do I need to start over?"

She handed me a damp rag. "Erase it with intention, and it should be fine."

"I'd rather not take chances." I dragged the cloth over the sigil, scrubbing off the chalk until the circle was clean. "This is why you should be doing this."

"You'll get it this time." She offered a smile, and I returned the gesture. One good thing about my little sis... She never stayed mad at me long.

I laid the phone in the circle and tried again. Ash nodded at each swoop and angle, and I paused at the bottom loop before bringing it left and completing the design.

"Perfect." She used my shoulder to push herself upright.

I stood, taking the phone and chalk with me and setting them on the table by the skull. The back door opened, and four sets of footfalls plodded toward us... my team, filing into the room. Chaos slid an arm around Ash's waist, and she rested her hand on his chest.

I really did feel bad for wishing her man away. Maybe someday I'd learn how to express things like that in words, but today was not that day. Instead, I turned to Shade. "That was fast."

"We're getting good at battling imps." He took off his knife holster and laid it on the table.

"It helps when you've got a demon they obey," Patrice said. "We convinced Inga that Chaos used a spell to control them, but now she wants the recipe."

"Luis and Madeline were there too." Shade curled his lip at the skull. "A few others showed up before we left, and they all but demanded you call a meeting."

"Maybe we should tell everyone what's going on." Miles peered at the sigil in the middle of the floor. "One demon we can hide, but two?"

"Absolutely not." I paced around the circle, turning at the top and retracing my path. "I will call a meeting to enlist their help, but *no one* is to know about the demons or the curse. Understood?"

Shade gave a mock salute, and the others nodded.

My phone chimed, and I closed my eyes, letting out a long exhale and steeling myself for whatever beastie had busted through this time. I swiped open the screen to find a message from Chrys's mom. "Crap. Ivy's here with the funeral home. Ash, come with me. The rest of you, stay here and keep the doors closed."

Ash followed me through the library and out the back door, where a pair of men in suits were pulling a stretcher out of a van. Ivy wore dark glasses, and her jet-black hair was piled on top of her head in a messy, curly bun.

She stepped onto the porch, and Ash hugged her. "I'm so sorry this happened."

Ivy sniffled. "Thank you for keeping her here. I don't... I don't know what got into her."

A demon got into her. She already knew that. I held the door open for the stretcher and slipped past them to lead the way toward the storage room. Ash and I stepped inside, standing against the wall to make room for the men, and Ivy hesitated in the doorway.

She removed her glasses, revealing red-rimmed eyes with puffy, dark circles, and she shuffled into the room. Gasping, she covered her mouth before a sob rolled up from somewhere deep in her soul.

Her legs wobbled as she stumbled toward her daughter's body. We'd covered Chrys with a dark blue sheet, which Ivy gingerly grasped and pulled down. Another sob ripped from her chest, her pain palpable, making Ash tear up.

Pressure built in the back of my eyes as Ivy kissed her daughter's forehead and covered her again. Her entire body trembled on a deep inhale, her hands curling into tight fists with her exhale. I couldn't begin to imagine how she must've felt.

"How could you let this happen?" She whirled

toward me, her expression livid and pained. "You're in charge of this coven. Her blood is on your hands."

My brows shot toward my hairline, and I straightened my spine. Guess I didn't have to imagine. "We did everything we could to save her."

She stepped toward me, pointing her finger accusingly. "You should have stopped her before any of this happened. She never should have had access to dark magic, let alone instructions for summoning a demon."

"Whoa." I raised my hands, palms toward her. "She didn't learn it from us."

"We should step outside so they can move her." Ash placed a hand on Ivy's shoulder.

She shrugged off her touch and moved toward me. "This is your fault, you incompetent, wannabe priestess. Your mother and Cinder never would have let this happen."

I ground my teeth, Ash's words echoing in my mind. *This is happening because of Mom and Cinder.* But I couldn't say that out loud.

Ivy shook her finger at me. "I don't know what killed them, but whatever it was, it should have happened to you." She pointed at Ash. "To both of you."

"That was uncalled for." Ash moved between us and gestured to the door. "Let's wait outside."

Ivy took one step toward the exit before spinning

around. "You should have paid more attention to what was happening in your coven."

I crossed my arms, my jaw ticking, my patience thinner than single-ply toilet paper. "She's your daughter. Maybe you're the one who should have paid more attention."

She gasped, fury sparking in her eyes, and I thanked the goddess our basement had a concrete floor because I had no doubt she'd have summoned the roots from every tree in Salem to tear me to shreds. "You..."

I should have shut my mouth right then, but my temper flared, rendering me unable to stop the words from flowing. "Don't *you* come into our house and accuse us. Chrys brought dark magic into this coven. *Your daughter* tortured and killed one of us for goddess knows what reason. She lied, she hid things from us, and she used us. I...we...had nothing to do with her decisions, but her upbringing sure as hell did."

Another gasp, and she pressed her hand to her chest. If she'd worn pearls, she would have clutched them.

"Ivy, please." One of the men from the funeral home, who had been silently watching the exchange, gently grasped her elbow and led her out of the room before she could piss me off anymore.

Ash closed her eyes for a long blink, shaking her head.

"What?" I snapped.

"She's a grieving mother, and you blamed her for her daughter's death."

"She accused me of teaching Chrys dark magic and then wished us both dead." I jerked my hand toward the doorway she'd left through, doing my best to keep my middle finger from jutting up. "I had to say something."

She sighed. "Of course you did."

I could tell from the tone of her voice she didn't approve of the way I'd said it, but I didn't want to argue. Should I have shifted the blame onto Ivy's shoulders? Probably not, but I also didn't have to stand there and let her accuse me of everything.

Yes, I should have been paying more attention. Yes, I might have noticed something off about Chrys's behavior if I'd thought about it. Yes, I had screwed up royally every chance I'd gotten through this entire ordeal.

That didn't mean I was responsible for the decisions Chrys made.

The man returned to the room. "She's waiting in the car. If you'll excuse us, we'll get out of your hair."

"Be my guest." I stepped into the hall with Ash and waited for them to load the body onto the stretcher. They wheeled her out the back door, and I locked it behind them.

"I told you everyone would blame me," I said as we made our way toward the studio.

Ash stopped outside the door and clutched my shoulders. "No one will blame you for the thinning veil, but they will blame you for what happens next if we don't give them a heads up so they can protect themselves."

I sucked in a massive breath and blew it out hard. "You're right. We need to call the meeting." I shoved the door open and stepped inside.

"How did it go?" Patrice clasped her hands over her chest.

"Don't ask." I picked up the skull and dropped it into a bag before handing it to Ash. "Shade, Miles, set up the emergency meeting. Mayhem will have to wait."

A low growl rumbled from Chaos's chest. "The longer he waits, the angrier he will become. Postponing this will only serve to make him harder to control."

I put my hands on my hips. "We managed you just fine, didn't we?"

CHAPTER 5
EMBER

"Her plan, it seems, was to take over both the Boston Society of Magic and Salem." I stood at the podium in the hotel meeting room, facing twenty-plus members of our coven and trying not to sweat. "She summoned the demon, attempting to harness his power to make it happen."

They sat silently, filling five rows of chairs beneath a small chandelier, as I explained everything that was going on.

Okay, not *everything*, obviously. If they knew Ash hadn't ended the curse, but instead *was* the curse, all hell would have broken loose...and we were dealing with enough of the Underworld already, thank you very much. Besides, my sister was fine so far, and she had a demon who could calm her instantly if she decided to go nuts.

As long as he didn't go nuts with her.

Honestly, of the three Holland sisters, Ash was the best one of us to bear this curse. I'd have already brought it to fruition. Not on purpose, of course, but I tended to act before I thought, and Ash was the opposite.

I stared over their heads at the plain beige wall behind them while they processed what I'd said. The carpet beneath their cushioned chairs, dark blue with a gray, swirly pattern, held flecks of glitter from some goddess-knew-what event that had happened earlier in the week.

Or hell...it could have happened six months ago. Glitter was the herpes of the craft world. You could never get rid of it.

"I don't understand why she would do this," Inga finally said from the second row.

"None of us do." I paced across the raised platform, turning on my heel and returning to the podium. "But the damage has been done, and we need your help to keep the beasties at bay and the humans in the dark until we can mend the veil."

"How are we supposed to mend it when the rifts are happening so fast?" Luis asked. "Why haven't you done it already?"

My jaw tightened, and I cut my gaze to Ash, who nodded her encouragement. I didn't need encouraging. I needed her to get up here and answer these questions before I said something I shouldn't.

Why hadn't we mended it already? Gee, why hadn't we just gone ahead and done it? "Don't you think we would have if we could? It's a complicated situation."

"It doesn't sound complicated." He crossed his arms. "Chrys thinned it by summoning the demon. She's dead, and the demon was vanquished. Unless there's more you aren't telling us..."

"There's nothing more." My nostrils flared as I ground my teeth. "We're working on it." Heat rose up my neck to climb across my cheeks, my other set of cheeks clenching so tightly I could have cracked a pecan.

"We have to find Cinder first." Ash stood and joined me behind the podium. "I've researched the phenomenon, and we need the power of three elemental witches to mend it properly."

Luis sat up straighter. "Isn't your boyfriend a fire witch?"

Ash looked at me, the poster child for the deer in the headlights expression.

"Three witches of the same bloodline," I said. "Same element, same blood, powerful spell that will drain our vim to the point of near death. It's complicated." And not entirely true, but whatever.

"Oh." He relaxed his accusing posture, and I let my

glutes return to their normal, unclenched state. "How do you know she's alive? She went missing months ago."

"We have reason to believe she is," Ash said.

"Reason which we can't divulge," I added before he could ask what.

We'd told so many lies since this started happening, both by omission and bald-faced, I couldn't keep up with them anymore. "While we're working on finding Cinder, we need you to be vigilant about the rifts. Binding and sealing potions are your friends, shadow spells when you can get them, distractions when you can't, and when in doubt, stab them through the heart."

I jumped off the platform and strode through the door before they could ask any more questions I couldn't answer honestly. Ten minutes later, my team filed out and met me at the van.

"Thanks for leaving us to handle the rest of the interrogation." Ash yanked the side door open and climbed inside. I slid into the driver's seat while Chaos, Shade, Miles, and Patrice filled the rest of the seats.

"It's all good." Shade lowered the visor to check his hair in the mirror, sliding his hand over his blond locks and smoothing them back toward his manbun. "I handled it. Next time, I can run the whole meeting if you need me to."

I caught Ash's eyeroll in the rearview mirror before I put the van in gear and headed home. I would never let Shade run a meeting, no matter how much his ego wanted to. Ash, on the other hand, would be much better at keeping the peace. Maybe next time.

Actually, I hoped to Hecate there wouldn't be a next time.

"They all seem to have bought the story that Chrys is to blame for everything," Patrice said as I pulled into the lot behind our building.

"And I don't plan to give them any more reasons to think otherwise." I put it in park and opened the door. "No more side quests. It's time for the next part of our plan."

We entered through the back door, passed through the library, and gathered in Ash's sigil studio. I motioned for Chaos to join me in front of the two grimoires I'd laid open on the table. "This is the one Ash used to contain Mayhem at the church." I pointed to the book we'd confiscated from Chrys. "And this is the one I used to contain you after we got you out of Ash's head." I pointed to our book. "Which do you recommend?"

He chuckled and closed the second book. "You did not contain me in that circle. I complied for Ash's sake."

I reopened it and flipped to the page in question. "It says it's for holding demons."

He shrugged. "Lower-level fiends, of course. Possibly some mid-level. There isn't much that can contain a Prince of Hell, but Chrys's spell can. It worked on me...several times, I'm ashamed to admit."

"Well, isn't that peachy?" I drummed my fingertips together, silently berating myself for choosing a weak spell when I was supposed to be saving Ash. Things could have gone *very* differently if Chaos hadn't already been enamored of my sister when we exorcized him.

As much as I'd hated their budding relationship in the beginning, we'd have been screwed hard and fast without it...and not in a fun way. But it didn't matter now. What was done was done and all that jazz.

"Let's do this thing." I shot flames from my fingertips to each of the candles on the floor.

Ash lit the ones on the tables and turned off the overhead lights. "It's a short incantation. Can everyone memorize it?"

I scanned the Latin on the page, committing it to memory before stepping out of the way so the others could do the same. Shade glanced at it quickly and nodded. "I still remember it from last time."

"Before we do this..." Patrice wrung her hands. "I don't understand why we can't summon them both at once. Get all three of them together so they can end the curse and we can mend the veil right now."

"Discord will not be easy to summon." Chaos took

Ash's hand and moved toward the circle. "Cinder freed him from the dark prison, so he owed his debt to her and no one else. He must be enticed to cross the veil again, and you will need Mayhem on your side to convince him to comply."

"And Mayhem is already the unhappiest camper I've ever met," Ash said. "You were busy with Chrys when we exorcized him, but let me tell you... He was pissed."

I stood on the opposite side of Chaos and grabbed his hand. "They're right. The longer we leave Mayhem in prison, the pissier he's going to be. Chaos needs to reason with him, make him understand the plan. Then we can convince Discord to bring Cinder and our parents back."

"Whatever it takes to set things straight so we can have some peace in Salem." Shade slapped his palm into mine, and Miles joined hands with Ash, both, once again, taking no issue with sharing a demon's power.

Patrice, ever the reluctant one, splayed her fingers before clenching her fists and splaying them again. "I should save my vim in case someone needs healing. You've all been using his magic more than any witch should."

My teeth click audibly, my grip on the guys' hands tightening with my frustration. I should have known better than to bring a healer on board and ask her to do anything but heal. Yes, we were light witches and consorting with demons went against our very nature, but sometimes even those closest to the goddess had to work in the gray areas to get things done.

"It's for the greater good," I said, my teeth still clenched tightly.

She inclined her chin. "It isn't right, and Hecate would agree."

I exhaled and yanked my hands free to press my fingers to my temples. I'd already brought her into the fold. She knew as much about the problem as the rest of us, and we would need her healing eventually. I couldn't send her packing like I wanted to, so I made a face at Ash that hopefully said *help me out here.*

My sister opened her mouth to speak, but Chaos beat her to it. "Hecate spends a great deal of time in the Underworld. Your goddess wouldn't be as opposed to my help as you might imagine."

Patrice jerked her head back as if she'd been slapped. "Don't speak ill of our goddess."

"I'm not speaking ill." Chaos held his hand toward me. "I'm simply stating a fact. Hecate exists in the gray areas. Dark witches worship her too."

"We need you, Patrice," Ash said. "I'll temper the demon magic. You'll hardly feel it."

I grabbed the guys' hands again. "If you don't help, he might break free and kill people. Do you want that on your conscience?"

Ash cut me a look, but Patrice gave her head a tiny shake and slipped her hand into Miles's. "This is the last time," she whispered.

I didn't mention the fact that we had another demon to summon after this. One step at a time. "Give it everything you've got. Mayhem has no loyalty to us, and he doesn't listen to reason from Chaos. No doubt he won't want to listen to us either, so we'll have to make him."

We recited the containment spell three times, and I hoped to Hecate we pronounced the Latin correctly. The air around us buzzed with magic, building with each recitation until the atmosphere thickened like pudding.

With one final push, we sent the magic into the circle, the candles flickering in response to our spell. The vibration in the room lifted, returning to normal, and we released our hands.

Patrice rubbed her palms on her pants. "I still felt it."

I fought an eye roll and turned to Chaos. "Test it."

He arched a brow, holding my gaze until I really did roll my eyes. "Test it, please?"

He reached toward the containment circle, his palm pressing against the invisible magic. "It will hold him. For how long, I can't be certain." He rested his other hand against the circle and shoved before nodding his approval.

I turned to the summoning spell and scanned the page. "I never thought I'd see the day when I willingly summoned a demon."

Shade clutched a dagger in each hand. "We're here for you."

But should they be? As acting High Priestess, it was my job to keep my coven safe. If something happened…if the circle didn't hold…Mayhem could kill us all. And then what? Salem would have two Princes of Hell on the loose and not a soul who knew what was happening.

Ash seemed convinced he wouldn't harm her as long as she bore Chaos's mark, but I had my doubts. If I had been imprisoned for centuries, rational thought would be tough to grasp.

I set the book next to the skull. "I want the three of you to wait upstairs during the summoning."

Shade laughed incredulously. "Not a chance."

I eyed the skull before pinning him with a steely glare. "I mean it. Take Miles and Patrice upstairs. Actually, you should all leave the building. Go have lunch or something."

"You can't be serious." Miles sheathed his daggers, concern etching lines on his forehead. "If he breaks free…"

"That's exactly why I want you out. This curse is on my family. It has nothing to do with you, and I won't risk your lives by exposing you to the hurricane we're about to unleash."

"Ember makes a good point," Chaos said. "When Mayhem materializes and sees five witches with their weapons drawn, he will assume you are threatening him, and he will act accordingly."

"They're right, guys." Ash nodded. "We have to reason with a livid demon. The fewer distractions, the better."

Shade glared at Ash and then at me. "Okay. We'll wait upstairs, but we'll be down at the first sign of struggle."

"I would expect nothing less." The tension in my shoulders eased a tiny bit. "Since you're staying upstairs, Patrice, can you bottle freezing and mending spells for the coven?"

"Of course." She nodded and hurried up the steps, no doubt relieved her presence wasn't required for the summoning.

"They'll need shadow magic too," I said. "Bottle as many as you can without overtaxing your vim.

Shade's jaw ticked, and Miles grasped his shoulder. "Come on. I'll help you."

The guys headed to the stairs, and Shade paused on the bottom step. "If you need help down here..."

"We'll let you know." I held my breath as their footsteps receded, and when the kitchen door opened, I exhaled hard. "Thanks for backing me up."

"It's the right thing to do." Ash picked up the skull and offered it to me.

Pinpricks gathered in my palms, spiraling up my arms the moment my skin touched bone. A shiver swirled through my body, making my arm hairs stand on end as I set it in the circle, centered over Mayhem's sigil.

Rubbing my hands together to dissipate the sensation, I returned to the table and grabbed the grimoire. "Let's invite a little Mayhem into our lives."

CHAPTER 6
MAYHEM

Time was meaningless in my dark prison. Each minute that passed could have been hours. Each day could have been a century. Every second of excruciating silence added fuel to the flames of my rage.

I ignored the faint tickle at the base of my head. Deprived of all my senses, my mind often fabricated sensations that could not be. I'd had no corporeal form since Isabel trapped me, taking my skull and vanquishing me to this fate worse than extinction.

My fury flared at the thought of the treacherous witch, the idea that Chaos now did another witch's bidding twisting the knife of betrayal.

The tickle intensified, spreading over my scalp and turning to pinpricks. It crawled through my essence like fingers jutting into my soul, threatening to shred the very fibers of my being.

In this fluid form, I did not breathe, yet my perceived lungs seized, collapsing on themselves, a crushing weight snapping ribs that did not exist. Words in an ancient tongue echoed in my mind, calling to me, coaxing me toward the veil.

My prison fought back, tightening around me like a boa squeezing the life from its prey. But the witches calling me were stronger than the one who imprisoned me. The magic holding me unraveled, and the new power sucked my spirit form through a tunnel of blinding light.

The veil, normally an iron wall, impassable for a creature of my level, tore open like a sheet of thin parchment. In the form of purple smoke, I poured through the rift.

My skull lay in the center of a summoning circle, atop my mark, which was perfectly drawn. Anticipation caused my energy to flash and spark, and I heard a faint gasp somewhere in the room. I paid the sound no mind as I billowed around my skull. Finally, after Hades knew how long, I would be reborn.

My energy intensified, and I spiraled like a funnel cloud, drawing my skull upward into my essence. Lightning cracked within the circle, my magic building, vibrating, creating flesh and bone.

My feet hit the floor, and a triumphant roar ripped

from my lungs. My gaze locked on the blue-haired witch, and I lunged, slamming into an invisible, magical wall. I roared again, this time lowering my head and ramming my horns against the circle.

The magic held.

"Release me." I glared at my brother. "Let me go, and I will spare her life."

"You and I both know that's a lie." Chaos crossed his arms. "But if you even attempt to harm my witch, the dark prison will feel like a vacation in paradise when I'm finished with you."

I would like to see him try. "Why did you summon me?"

"We need your help," Ash said.

I glanced at her, dragging my gaze down her form. I saw nothing special about the woman who had entranced my brother. Aside from the color of her hair, her features were unremarkable. "Did you not learn from our previous encounter with a witch who needed our help?"

"These women are not Isabel. They won't betray us like she did." He slid his arm behind her waist, pulling her to his side to drive his traitorous point home.

My hands curled into the tightest fists my talons would allow. "Release me."

"We will when you learn how to behave," the

purple-haired witch said, and I focused on her for the first time.

Titling my head, I studied the woman. She wore tight black pants over her long, slender legs, and a matching shirt clung to her curves, reminding me of how long it had been since I'd felt a woman's touch.

I tore my gaze away, lest I become entranced like my idiot brother. "How long was I imprisoned?"

"Nearly four centuries," he said.

It had felt like an eternity. "And you?"

"The same. I've only been free for a few weeks, and we are running out of time."

I scoffed. "Time is irrelevant to an immortal."

"The veil is thinning," Ash said. "In a few more weeks, there'll be nothing left to separate this world from yours."

"A problem not of my concern." I slammed my shoulder against the circle, and the magic pushed back, vibrating through my muscles and making my skin crawl. "Who created this ring?"

"We all did," the purple-haired witch said, "and if you don't learn how to be a good little demon, you'll never get out of it."

"Ember..." Ash said, warning drawing out her words.

They *all* did. I pressed my palms against the invisible wall. Perhaps these women weren't as powerful as I once suspected. Allowing the magic to seep into my skin, I sorted through the essence of each witch who cast it. Three lesser vibrations consorted with three more of immense power. I disregarded the lesser and focused on the latter.

When the magic registered in my psyche, I jerked away, fuming at what I'd discovered. "Traitor," I growled and jabbed my talons into the circle, hoping to tear it apart. The energy pulsed but did not give.

"You aided *five* witches to entrap me?" I thrust my horns against the wall, punched, and kicked. Still it held strong. "You will pay for what you've done, brother. Lucifer *will* hear of this."

Ember had the audacity to laugh. "So basically..." she chortled. "You're threatening to run home and tell your demon daddy that your brother hurt your feelings."

"Insolent witch!" I roared and pounded against the circle. How dare a mortal ridicule Mayhem. "I will kill you all."

She shook her head, crossing her arms over her chest as she took two overconfident steps toward me. "We've already exorcized and vanquished you once. You think we won't do it again?"

"Seriously, Em." Ash grabbed her arm. "Can we *not* provoke just one demon?" She looked at me. "The sooner you calm down and listen, the sooner you'll be free. We're on the same side, believe it or not."

"I will never be on a witch's side." I roared again,

the sound building in my gut and belting out at a decibel loud enough to shatter their eardrums. The witches clutched the sides of their heads, their knees buckling beneath them as I continued my auditory assault.

"Mayhem, stop," Chaos demanded.

I roared even louder.

CHAPTER 7

EMBER

The walls and floor shook with Mayhem's scream. The sound brought Ash and me to our knees, and covering my ears did nothing to relieve the sensation of daggers stabbing my brain. I stumbled to my feet and lunged toward the table to grab Ash's satchel. Yanking it down by the strap, I returned to the floor, where Chaos kneeled beside her, shouting at his brother to stop.

"Tell me you have a silencing spell in there." I slid the bag toward her.

"What?" she shouted.

I stuck my fingers in my ears and mouthed *silencing spell* before gesturing to the offending demon. She nodded and rummaged through the bag, pulling out a small pink bottle triumphantly.

I uncorked it, grabbed her hand to give her as

much vim as she needed, and hurled the contents into Mayhem's face. "Sound offending, words unending, we call on the goddess to make the noise cease," we said in unison. As the particles gathered around his throat, the magic cut off his roar, casting the room into glorious silence.

Well, silence except for the ringing in my ears and the sound of footsteps pounding down the stairs.

"What the hell was that?" Shade shouted as he and Miles raced into the studio.

"Shh..." I covered my ears, wincing at the sound. "Give us a minute."

My head pounded with the high-pitched tone assaulting both my ears, but I rose to my feet and turned toward the culpable demon as Chaos helped Ash stand.

Mayhem stood nearly eight feet tall, with more muscles rippling beneath his dark purplish-gray skin than I ever thought possible. Thick horns with a spiral texture jutted outward from the sides of his head before arching up like a bull's, and a set of what I could only call tusks protruded from both his upper and lower jaws.

Aside from his bad attitude and unnecessary volume, he was a magnificent sight to see. Thighs, thicker than my waist, led down to cloven hooves, and upward...

I squeezed my eyes shut and turned to Shade. No

way would I allow myself to find that *thing* attractive. He was a monster. A creature from Hell, for Hecate's sake.

"That was Mayhem feeling powerless and yelling like weak men tend to do when no one wants to listen to them." I glanced at the demon again, and he pounded his chest, no doubt shouting at the top of his lungs for us to set him free.

"Damn." Miles looked Mayhem up and down. "He's big."

Ash shrugged. "No bigger than Chaos. Will you go up and ask Patrice for some headache powder and something to stop the ringing in our ears? I'd rather not waste my vim on another spell right now."

"Sure." He bounded upstairs while Shade eyed Mayhem.

"I guess he doesn't want to cooperate?" He moved closer to the containment circle, and the demon slammed his shoulder against the magic, making it pulse. Shade flinched.

"Nope." I rubbed my temples to counter the pressure in my skull. "If he would just listen, he'd understand how we can help each other."

Shade tilted his head. "Doesn't he owe you a favor since you freed him?"

"Indeed he does." Chaos tugged Ash to his chest and rubbed her head tenderly. "And that favor should be to break Ash's curse."

"But we need Discord for that, so for now, we have to figure out how to tame the savage beast." I pressed my thumb between my eyes, but it didn't ease the pain.

Miles finally came down and handed Ash and me each a steaming mug. "She put both powders into one drink and said you need to take it all at once."

I hadn't planned to sip the stuff. Tipping my head back, I chugged the bitter, nearly boiling-hot potion. It burned all the way down to my stomach, and if fire wasn't my element, I'd have been scorched. Instead, a coolness spread through my body, quieting the ring and easing the splitting pain in my head to a dull, manageable ache.

"I guess Patrice is still afraid of a couple of hellions?" I set the mug on the table and wiped my mouth with the back of my hand.

Miles shrugged and gave a tiny nod. "How long will the silencing spell last on him?"

I eyed the demon, my gaze dropping to his unmentionables three times before I managed to hold his gaze. In my defense, I wasn't the only one having trouble not looking at his junk. Miles, Shade, and even Ash's gaze bounced up and down his nakedness.

With a package that impressive, it was hard not to look.

I took a deep breath and blew it out hard, a wave of fatigue washing over me, though I'd had plenty of time to recharge after this morning's battle. If I wanted to be introspective, I could have admitted it was mental and emotional fatigue. But I was the fighter, the warrior. My brain didn't get tired because I used my body more.

"We just want to have a civilized chat." I parked my hands on my hips. "I think we've demonstrated our power enough, and we have Chaos on our side. If you want out of this circle, you need to listen to what we have to say."

His nostrils flared and the tendons in his neck tightened, but at least he kept his mouth shut.

"We will remove the silencing spell if you promise not to try busting our eardrums again. Can you use your big boy words and talk like a grownup?"

"That's not helpful, Em," Ash muttered. "Don't patronize him."

"He deserves a lot worse." I arched a brow at him, and he narrowed his deep-purple, soul-penetrating eyes.

"It's the only way to gain your freedom," Chaos said.

Mayhem's gaze bounced from his brother to each of us before he settled on me and spread his hands as if conceding.

"Now we're getting somewhere." My sword lay on the table, and I caressed the skull pommel before running my fingers over the rosewood handle. "Ash will undo the silencing spell, but if you try anything at all, I will lob off your head and vanquish you back to your prison for another four hundred years."

My sister made a disapproving sound with her throat, but I ignored her. I'd dealt with plenty of men like Mayhem at Spellbound Axe. Maybe they weren't demonic, but eighty percent of our clientele consisted of testosterone-laden Neanderthals who thought drinking beer, throwing sharp objects, and proclaiming themselves alpha males would make them so. In reality, they were just insecure assholes, and the best way to put them in their place was to exert your own dominance.

Mayhem was no different.

Ash looked from me to Chaos, who nodded, and she recited the undoing spell. "What I've done is now undone. As I will it, so mote it be."

The moment the silencing spell lifted, a growl rumbled in Mayhem's chest, his lips pulling up into a sneer.

"Ah-ah." I held up a finger. "We're in control of this situation."

"We'll see for how long." He arched a challenging brow.

I picked up my sword and spun it at my side before clutching it in both hands. "Okay. Back to prison you go."

"Ember!" Ash scolded, but I lifted it, ready to swing.

"Wait." Mayhem held up his hands in surrender. "Perhaps we can make a deal."

"No deals. Demons lie." I adjusted my grip. "Bind him, Shade."

"Gladly." He picked up a freezing spell and popped the cork.

"Brother..." Disbelief widened Mayhem's eyes.

Chaos crossed his arms. "These witches aren't to be trifled with. I've never met another who possessed such power."

He backed away from the circle's edge, his eyes calculating. "I will hear what you have to say."

"Good choice." Shade recapped the potion. "I would not want to be on Ember's bad side. The woman's got a temper."

I smirked. "Only because you love to piss me off."

Mayhem stretched his neck, his vertebrae popping and cracking like industrial-strength bubble wrap. "Tell me, witch. What spell have you used to entrance and enslave my brother?"

I returned my sword to the table and leaned against the edge, crossing my legs at the ankles. "She didn't use a spell. It's all L-O-V-E love."

He let out a scoff of disbelief and shook his head at Chaos. "Is this true?"

"It's fate." Chaos rested his hand on Ash's back.

A growl rumbled in Mayhem's chest. "Doubtful."

"She summoned me accidentally, not knowing my mark was demonic." He pressed his lips to the side of her head. "What else could it be?"

Mayhem scoffed. "Accidents do not mean fate."

"She summoned me without my skull."

Surprise lifted his dark brow. "Impossible."

"Yet here I stand. Ash is the victim of Isabel's curse..." He dropped his hand and stepped toward the circle.

"These are Holland witches?" Mayhem asked, his deep, rumbly voice tinged with disbelief.

Chaos nodded. "Ash is the third born, the bearer of the hex, and only we have the power to break it."

Mayhem narrowed his eyes at Ash, his gaze flicking between my sister and her demon. "It's impossible without Discord."

"Our sister is already taking care of that." I pushed from the table and stepped toward him. "She summoned him, and he took her to Hell to find our parents. The gears are already in motion, and you were the final cog in our wheel."

"What makes you believe I will comply?"

I lifted a shoulder dismissively, and his gaze followed the movement. "You don't have a choice. If you refuse to help us, I'll send you back to prison. We've already vanquished you, a shedim, a horde of imps, and a chicken snake. It won't be difficult."

He stepped toward me. "A chicken snake?"

"A basilisk," Ash said. "And don't forget the fae scout."

My muscles crawled beneath my skin at the memory. "An overgrown cockroach with nearly impenetrable armor. Ever met one? They're nasty."

He curled his lip. "I despise the fae."

"Don't we all?" I matched his expression. Well, I curled my lip anyway. Without the tusks and protruding brow, I couldn't mimic him identically.

Chaos tapped a finger against his thigh, as if formulating a plan. "With the veil this thin, there could be an uprising brewing. If we don't mend it, and they take over this world, ours will be next."

A look passed between the demons that I didn't dare try to decipher. Could there be an uprising brewing? Why else would they send a scout across the veil if not to check out our realm?

Hecate have mercy, we did not have time for side quests.

"A war with the fae..." Mayhem's dark eyes brightened. "You should have led with that. I'm always willing to kill those maddening creatures. When do we begin?"

"Hold that thought." I raised a finger. "I need a word with my team."

I jerked my head toward the door, and Ash, Miles, and Shade slipped through. "You too, Chaos."

We joined the others in the library, and I pulled the door shut. "Do you really think the fae are planning an attack, or were you just blowing smoke?"

"Both," Chaos said. "Mayhem's favorite pastime is killing the fae that attempt to enter our world. If he believes he'll get to battle them here, he is more likely to conform to our strategy."

I paced in front of Ash's desk. "But you think they might really have a plan to attack?"

Ash wrinkled her nose. "The scout did say 'our world now.' I doubt he meant he was going home."

I dragged a hand down my face. "Goddess, help us."

"Hopefully we can find Cinder and Discord and fix the veil before that happens," Miles said.

Ash lowered her gaze. "Hopefully." The sadness in her voice made my heart ache, but it had to be done.

"One thing at a time." I continued pacing. "If acting like we're about to go to war with the fae will make Mayhem join our side, then that's what we'll do."

"Is it safe to come down?" Patrice called from the top of the stairs.

"Not quite." She would shit a cinder block if she saw Mayhem in his demon form. Chaos scared her enough. "We need him to transform. Where are you keeping Chaos's clothes?"

"I'll go up and get him something." Ash ascended the steps, and the rest of us returned to the studio.

The moment I opened the door, Mayhem slammed his meaty shoulder against the circle, making it pulse. A glimmer of opal crawled across the invisible wall, the first sign of the magic weakening. I cocked my head, lifting a brow in warning, and he narrowed his eyes, a growl rumbling in his chest.

"What did I say about trying to break free?" I picked up my sword and tested its weight, spinning it from side to side. "We have to be able to trust you. To trust each other."

He exhaled a humorless laugh. "I will never trust a witch."

"You can trust I'll lob your head clean off the second I sense your betrayal."

He crossed his arms, making his biceps bulge. "You talk in circles, witch. I tire of your repetition."

I opened my mouth for a comeback, but the beastie had a point. I could only threaten him so many times before I either acted on it or the threat became hollow. "First rule of existing in this realm: You have to be in human form, so go ahead and make that happen."

He scowled. "I was summoned to this realm long before you existed. I know the rules of your world."

"A lot has changed since then," Chaos said.

"Humans fear witches as much as demons." He

rested his hands on his hips, drawing my gaze to his donkey-sized ding dong and reminding me just how long it had been since I'd... Well, you know.

I turned to put my sword on the table to stop myself from staring. "Most humans don't know witches are real. Not ones like us with actual powers. The ones that do also know we are the people who keep Salem safe from your kind."

"It's your kind who summons mine. If they knew who the real threat was..."

I closed my eyes and pressed my lips into a thin line. I wasn't the only one keeping this conversation on the merry-go-round. "Will you please transform into the least menacing version of yourself so we can go kick some fae ass?"

"We could use your insight," Shade said. "Their scout nearly took out our best fighter."

I snapped my head toward him, ready to berate him. I handled Roachman just fine, thank you very much.

"My insight in exchange for my freedom. I accept those terms."

"Nope." I raised my hands. "I drew your sigil. The debt you owe is to me, and I want you to break my sister's curse."

"As do I, brother," Chaos said.

Mayhem cut his gaze between the three of us, his eyes calculating. "Agreed."

He said the word, but something about his expression told me freeing him wouldn't make our lives any easier. Curling his hands into fists, he strained, tightening his jaw as purple smoke billowed around him, filling the containment circle until the beast inside was no longer visible.

Something cracked—maybe his neck?—and the thick cloud swirled around him before vanishing as quickly as it had formed.

Miles gasped, Shade swallowed hard, and me...? My ovaries might have exploded at the sight.

He stood maybe an inch or two shorter than Chaos, which put him at around six-foot-three. He had black hair, wavy on top and short on the sides, with a matching goatee and piercing, deep-set, otherworldly blueish-lavender eyes.

I could have bounced a crystal off his pecs if not for the dark hair sprinkled across his flawless skin. A trail of it led downward, over defined abs cut into an eight-pack. Or was it ten? I didn't have time to count because my gaze dipped lower, against my will, and locked on his package.

Good goddess. Why did I have a sudden craving for sausage?

Muscular thighs completed his statue-perfect appearance, and I finally tore my gaze away from his lower half to meet his eyes. He smirked, the expression both amused and menacing at the same time.

He spread his hands. "Not what you expected?"

Looks-wise, I wasn't surprised in the least. He was hot as hellfire, like his brother; part of his arsenal to prey on the weak, as demons liked to do.

What I did not expect was the visceral reaction my body had at the sight of him. Parts of me clenched while other parts tingled; warmth spread through my abdomen, though a chill cascaded down my spine, all of it coming together in a *wowzers I need some of that.*

I *so* did not need any of that, but damn. I knew who I'd be dreaming about tonight.

"Got the clothes." Ash slipped through the door and laughed. "And he's got you all entranced."

I blinked and shook my head, chasing away the naughty thoughts that had taken up residence in my brain. One Holland sister getting down with a demon was enough. Mayhem was a means to an end. Nothing more.

Ash handed me the clothes, dark jeans and a t-shirt. No underwear. Did Chaos go commando? I shook my head again and chunked the garments at Mayhem's head. He caught them before they reached their target...demon reflexes and whatnot.

"Put those on, and I'll break the circle." My eyes finally obeyed the command from my brain, and my gaze remained on his face as he bent down to step into the jeans. When he pulled on the shirt, the tension in my jaw loosened, but it would take a cold shower to rid myself of the unwanted hormones coursing through my veins.

I eyed the salt ring surrounding him and glanced at Chaos, who nodded. Ash rested a hand on my shoulder and said, "It's time."

My stomach tightened, my insides tying into nauseating knots. Once he'd gotten his hissy fit out of the way, he'd become compliant with all my requests. I had to hold up my end of the bargain.

Locking my gaze on his eyes, I stepped toward the circle. "Do not make me regret this."

CHAPTER 8
MAYHEM

The moment the witch swiped her boot through the salt circle, my senses came alive. The high vibrations of their light magic raised the hairs on my skin, and the scents of herbs and chemicals assaulted my nostrils. My nose twitched at the stench.

My brother kept a protective arm wrapped around his witch, but the one they called Ember and the two males stood tense, ready to draw their weapons at the first sign of my malice. I held in a laugh.

If Chaos weren't here, I could take the four of them out before they had a chance to call on their magic or swing a sword. Instead, I would bide my time, make them believe they could command me like they did my brother, and when his guard was down...then I would strike with a force they couldn't begin to imagine.

I stepped out of the circle and inhaled deeply, my face contorting as the pungent odor burned my nasal passages and throat. "What is that sharp, offending stench?"

Ash and Ember looked at each other, the former shaking her head before the latter said, "What stench?"

"I believe he means the smells of bleach and the other products you use in your home," Chaos said. "The scent is one that didn't exist when we last visited this realm."

Ember made an uncouth snorting sound through her nose. "You're offended by the smell of clean? Why doesn't that surprise me?"

Her boldness of speech and coarse mannerisms would have caused her imprisonment when last I was here, yet something about her brashness intrigued me. She seemed wild, untamed, and I wondered how many men had tried to put her in her place and failed.

I raked my gaze down her form, taking in her slender curves, imagining the feel of her skin beneath my fingertips. If she were any being other than a witch, she would be mine by the end of the day. Taming this shrew would be easier than teaching Cerberus to sit. She would do my bidding whenever and wherever I chose.

But witches were the vilest of creatures, and the

mere thought of bedding one made my stomach turn. I would never make that mistake again.

"My eyes are up here, sweetheart," she said, and I flicked my gaze to hers.

"I haven't seen a woman's bosom in centuries. It's unfortunate my first had to be yours." I started toward the door, but Chaos blocked my exit. The male witches flanked him as if they stood a chance of keeping me from my destination.

"First of all..." Ember's voice drew my attention, and I turned to her as she continued, "Nobody says bosom anymore. You need to watch a few hours of television to get up to speed on modern vernacular."

I had no clue what she was talking about, but I didn't dare admit my ignorance to a witch. Instead, I simply crossed my arms. "Noted."

Her nostrils expanded, and she angled her head while clenching her jaw until the tendons in her neck protruded. Fisting her hands, she tipped her head toward the ceiling and paced a short distance before returning and pacing again.

"And second?" I asked.

She stilled and faced me. "What second?"

"Generally, when someone precedes a statement with the phrase 'first of all,' there is something else they intend to say."

She scoffed. "Are you kidding me right now?"

I arched a brow, happy to goad her, though I

couldn't fathom why she questioned my seriousness. "Not in the slightest."

She splayed her fingers, her gaze cutting to the sword lying on the table next to her. "Chaos..." she said through clenched teeth. "Get a handle on your brother before I do something I shouldn't. I need some air." She grasped her sword and marched past me, her shoulder purposely hitting my arm on her way to the door.

"Give us a minute." My brother pressed his lips to Ash's forehead, and she nodded before gesturing for the males to join her outside.

When the door closed, I turned a livid gaze to Chaos. "I should stab you through the heart and ask Lucifer to smother you in the tarpits for what you've done."

He shook his head, his expression one of pity. "I would vanquish you before you lifted a talon. Brother, you need to understand..."

"I understand enough. You've fallen victim to yet another witch's wiles, and when she's done with you, she'll send you back to the dark prison without a second thought."

He exhaled hard, closing his eyes much longer than a blink. "Who's the one talking in circles now?"

I opened my mouth to argue, but my words would be useless. The conviction in his voice said he believed in this fantasy with every fiber of his being. For the first time since my fury flared over his involvement, I felt something else.

Pity. The great and powerful Chaos had been enticed...tricked...once again. Perhaps he wasn't as intelligent as he claimed to be.

He spread his hands to his sides. "You know as well as I do what would happen if the veil collapsed. It's our duty as Princes of the Underworld to maintain the balance between realms."

"You speak of duty, yet you play house with a witch."

"This development surprised me as much as it enrages you, but who am I to question fate?" He leaned against the table, crossing his arms. "You'll be happy to hear that the only way we can mend the veil is by returning to Hell. With Discord's help, we'll repair it on our side while the Holland sisters take care of theirs. We'll be home soon, and you'll never see these witches again."

His eyes tightened as if the mere thought of leaving this world pained him, and I shifted my gaze to the sigil so carefully drawn on the floor. "Tell me more about the fae invading this realm."

"Swarms of lesser fae have been breaking through for weeks. This morning, we encountered and killed a scout, which makes me believe the greater fae are planning to invade. They will decimate the human population if we allow it to happen. Do you want the fae to control two realms?"

"Perhaps we should slaughter the humans first and claim this realm for demonkind."

"Lucifer would never allow it. You know he relies on the souls of the damned to fuel Hell. Our only choice is to help this coven protect their world...and to end Isabel's curse."

My lip curled at the mention of the wicked woman's name.

"Think of what she did to us," Chaos said. "Do you want to allow the curse to come to fruition when she never paid the price?"

I waved a hand, dismissing his question. "We will find her descendants and make them pay. Once Discord joins us, they'll be easy to identify."

"On that we can agree. The price will be paid for her betrayal, but our contract with her is null. I have no intention of letting her win. Do you?"

"You make a good point, brother. I will help you end the curse, but know that it is out of spite, not for your little witch."

And once the curse was broken, then I would get my revenge.

CHAPTER 9
EMBER

"It's too quiet in there." I leaned toward the closed door, straining to hear the demons. "I think they left through the storefront."

"No, they didn't." Ash grabbed my wrist before I could turn the knob. "Chaos wouldn't let Mayhem roam free, trust me."

"He better not." Fighting the urge to bust in and check, I strode to her desk and sat on the edge. "What is it with him, anyway? It's like he's singled me out to be the one he hates when I didn't do a damn thing to him. In fact, I'm the one who drew his sigil. He should be thanking me, not pissing me off."

Ash pressed her lips together. "You haven't exactly been nice to him either."

"Why would I? He's..." I started to say *a demon* but

thought better of it. See? I could learn. "He's insufferable. Infuriating."

"He's been in prison for four hundred years," Miles said. "Maybe cut him some slack."

"Maybe I'll cut off his balls."

Ash laid a heavy hand on my shoulder. "Let's put Mayhem's castration on the back burner for now and focus on our next steps. We can't do this without him."

"Ash is right," Shade said. "I don't trust the guy, but we have to at least pretend to get along if we're going to save Salem."

"I will never get used to you two agreeing." The door opened, and I shot to my feet. Chaos crossed the threshold first, striding to Ash and clutching her hand as if he had to remind his brother of their connection.

Mayhem entered the library next, his posture cocky as hell, his expression... Honestly, I couldn't read it all, but his calculating eyes raking up and down my body made my blood run cold everywhere except my nether region.

Damn demons and their damn sexy human forms.

"I need shoes and a few hours with your television so I can acclimate myself to the current century."

I almost told him people in Hell need ice water, but that idiom didn't seem appropriate, seeing as how he *was* from Hell. Instead, I held my tongue, glanced at his feet, and tugged my wallet from my back pocket.

"Miles, can you buy him a pair of size twelves?" I handed him my credit card.

"How do you know that size will fit?" Mayhem curled his lip. "Don't witches have to cast spells for everything they do?"

I stiffened, scrambling for a good comeback, but Ash answered for me, "She worked at a shoe store for five years. If she says you're a twelve, you're a twelve."

Miles slipped my card into his pocket. "Got it. Anything else?"

"Undergarments," Mayhem said. "The seam of these trousers chafes my—"

"Get them a pack of undies." I tried to stop the image of the demon's junk from playing in my mind, but it was no use. He had some really nice junk.

"On it." Miles headed for the back door.

"Shade, go with him," I said.

His chest inflated as he cut his gaze between the demons. "I'm not an errand boy."

Good goddess, I did not have the patience for his ego. "Are you not a team player, either?" I cocked my head. "We don't go anywhere alone until this fiasco is sorted."

Mayhem laughed. "Consider yourself a babysitter, if it makes you feel better."

Shade's mouth tightened, and he inclined his chin, giving me the stink eye before turning on his heel and following Miles out the back. I would've loved to say my tension eased when the ego left the building, but the bare-foot, undie-less demon standing next to me exuded enough to make Shade seem like a shy puppy.

I pinched the bridge of my nose. "How can today not be over yet?"

"A few more hours, and it will be." Ash headed for the stairs. "Let's go up, and I'll order us dinner."

The demons walked behind Ash, and I took up the rear to make sure Mayhem didn't turn and bolt. Patrice stood in the kitchen, and the moment we walked through the door, her eyes widened, the bottle she held slipping from her hands and shattering on the floor.

"Oh! Umm." She kneeled, her gaze never straying from the guys as she picked up a shard of glass. "Ow! Dammit."

Blood pooled on her fingertip, and she hurried to the sink to rinse it. She had turned our kitchen into a healer's workshop, with dried herbs hanging in the window, bottles of spells lined up against the back-splash, and bowls and utensils spread across the countertop.

"I'll clean that up. Where are Miles and Shade?" She applied a styptic powder to her wound before wrapping it in a bandage.

"I've got it." Ash grabbed the broom and dustpan

from the pantry and swept up the mess. "They're buying shoes and clothes for Mayhem."

"Okay." Her gaze bounced between the demons.

"He's not going to hurt you." I cast Mayhem a challenging glare.

He arched a brow in return. "Not tonight anyway."

"I know." She wiped the counter with a rag, pink flushing her cheeks. "I set up a ward on the stairs. Well...more like an alarm for anyone with ill intent. I've mixed so many potions, my vim is a little taxed."

"Ember and I will set up more before we go to bed." Ash returned the broom to the pantry and swiped open her phone. "How do tacos sound?"

My stomach growled at the mere mention of nature's most perfect food. "Throw in a twelve-pack of Corona, and I'm sold."

"On it." Ash sank into the middle cushion on the sofa. "I'll ask the guys to pick it up on their way back.

Chaos gestured for her to slide over, and he took the middle seat before motioning for Mayhem to join them. "I found reality shows to be the best way to learn the current culture." He turned on the TV, and I climbed onto a stool at the counter.

"I'm meeting Inga outside to give her the spells." Patrice loaded a canvas bag with bottled magic. "I'd like to spend the night with her if that's okay. It'll free up a bed for..." Her gaze flicked to Mayhem.

I couldn't say I blamed her. I'd rather not sit here with an untamed demon in the house either, but I didn't have the option to leave. "No problem. I'll text you in the morning to touch base."

"Good luck sleeping." She flashed a hesitant smile before turning to the sink and washing the dishes she'd used.

I wouldn't need any luck at all to sleep tonight. Chaos seemed to have a handle on his brother, I had enough vim to set up some good alarms, and my reflexes when I first woke up were fast enough to behead Prince Pissy Pants in a heartbeat if he set them off. Plus, I was so damn tired I had no doubt I'd pass out the second my head hit the pillow.

Patrice left to meet Inga, and twenty minutes later, the guys returned with shopping bags, two dozen foil-wrapped tacos, and the beer.

"At last." Mayhem ripped open the pack of under-wear and dropped his drawers in the middle of the living room.

I tried to look away. I really did, but damn. "Lesson one, dude. We don't show the world our naughty bits. From now on, change in the bathroom."

"You've already seen my 'naughty bits,' so what's the problem?" He pulled on the undies and stepped into his jeans.

"Just…" I squeezed my eyes shut. "Keep watching TV so you can learn."

Miles handed out the food, and Shade set the twelve-pack on the coffee table. We all grabbed a beer, and Ash ate on the couch with the demons while Mayhem absorbed an episode of *Big Brother*.

Miles and Shade joined me at the table, and I popped the cap off my beer, taking a long pull and sinking deeper into my chair. The crisp, effervescent liquid tickled on its way to my stomach, and I let out a massive sigh.

Sadly, it was not a contented one. At the rate we were going, I might never experience that sensation again.

I took a bite of taco number one and closed my eyes, focusing on the flavor explosion of *al pastor*, cilantro, and chopped onions. The second bite of spicy, seasoned pork tasted better than the first, and before I knew it, I'd downed three tacos and moved on to my second beer.

"I guess Patrice is done playing with monsters?" Shade wiped his mouth with a paper towel.

"She's helping Inga," Ash said around a mouthful of pork.

"Nobody gets to bow out until this is through." I stood and tossed my wrappers into the trash. "Which is why we need to summon Discord ASAP. Hopefully we can fix this before any more overgrown insects break through and make the situation worse."

"Can we create a strong enough containment circle without Patrice?" Miles asked.

"I don't think she contributed much." Ash joined us at the table, leaving the demons with the TV. "I withheld as much of Chaos's magic from her as I could, and she didn't share much with us. She's truly afraid of them."

"Can you blame her?" Miles grabbed a second beer and popped the top. "She's a healer. We can't turn her into a fighter."

"We'll make it work." I tossed my empty bottle into the recycle bin. "Right now, we need to set up wards on the hall and bedroom doors. Nothing with ill intent gets into our rooms."

"What about out?" Shade leaned toward me, lowering his voice. "You're not afraid he'll take off while we sleep?"

"I'll stay up with him," Chaos said from the living room. "Recharge your vim in peace."

"Works for me." Yes, it went against my very nature to trust a demon, but Chaos had proved his loyalty to Ash a thousand times over. He might not have given a flying flip about me, but he wanted to save my sister as much as I did.

I grabbed a handful of crystals from the drawer, and Ash helped me set up the wards. Of course, I knew now that the ones I used against Chaos wouldn't have stopped him if he really wanted through, but I made sure to cast ones with alarms so I'd have a second to wake up if things went south.

With our protections in place, I headed for the shower, and just like I suspected, I was dead to the world as soon as my head hit the pillow. I could have slept a full twelve hours if not for the woman's agonizing wail ripping through the morning fog.

CHAPTER 10
MAYHEM

A tormented screech of pain sliced through the quiet morning, and I tilted my head toward the sound. "I haven't heard a scream like that since Lucifer tried to keep a banshee as a pet. Is it a normal occurrence here?"

"Not at all." Chaos shot to his feet and darted down the hallway, no doubt running to his witch's side to protect her.

I pulled on the size twelve boots Ember was certain would fit, nodding my approval when they did. Her talent would be useless most of the time, but it had come in handy today. Rising, I prepared to make my escape when Ember stormed into the living room.

She wore baggy pants, which, from my six hours with the television, I had learned were called sweats. A cropped t-shirt left her midsection exposed, and she tucked her disheveled purple hair behind her ear before stepping into the combat-style boots she'd left by the door.

"What happened out there?" she asked.

"How would I know? I've been inside the entire time."

"Ever heard of a window?" She yanked a cord, raising the blinds and filling the room with pale morning light. "Shit. And Patrice is twenty minutes away. Ash, guys, let's go."

The others filed out of the hall, stumbling as they put on shoes and strapped weapons to their bodies. "What's going on?" Shade asked as he tied his blond hair back in a band.

"Someone is bleeding out on the street." Ember pointed at me. "You stay here."

I laughed. "Not a chance."

She made a face at my brother, her mouth tight, her eyes strained.

"I will watch him." Chaos motioned toward the door.

Her mouth twitched as she blew out a hard breath. "Cloak us the second we step outside, Shade. Sound too. Ash, grab a couple bottles of shadow in case we have to split up."

Her sister did as she was told, and we hurried down the stairs and out the back door, my heart pumping with an excitement I hadn't felt in centuries.

Natural fog blanketed the ground outside, but as I stepped onto the sidewalk, another mist gathered around us, turning the already-desaturated world into shades of gray. Fire, healing, shadow magic... What did Miles bring to the team, I wondered. With his stormy gray eyes and jet-black hair, I would guess he could control some type of energy. Lightning, perhaps?

We exited the alley behind the witches' home and followed the path toward the one responsible for the scream. A crowd had gathered around the woman, making it difficult to see her injuries.

The witches paced the perimeter in search of the culprit while Ash attempted to peer through the crowd. "Do you sense anything demonic?" she asked my brother.

He inhaled deeply, searching the area for the tell-tale low vibration, and I did the same. "Nothing," he said before looking at me.

"I agree. It's probably a case of human-on-human violence. They rarely need much coaxing from our kind."

Sirens wailed in the distance, and the other witches returned to the scene. "Shade, uncloak me so I can elbow my way through the crowd," Ember said.

There was no need for that. I called on my mind power, bringing it to the surface after four hundred years of inactivity. The base of my skull buzzed with power...what people in this century called electricity...

and I sent my magic toward the two men standing closest to us.

The one in blue turned to the one in brown and landed a punch to his jaw. Brown fought back, slamming his fist into Blue's stomach, and the crowd backed away, giving the men room to brawl and the witches ample space to examine the victim.

"Chaos!" Ember snapped, her jaw tightening.

He raised his hands in a show of innocence before pointing at me. "I cause confusion. He causes violence."

She glared at me, a mesmerizing fire sparking in her eyes. "Stop it right now. This is not how we operate."

I pulled my magic away from the men and focused it on a woman. She slapped the man standing next to her. Ash and Miles kneeled by the bloody victim on the ground, finally having room to reach her, thanks to me.

Ember drew her sword, clutching it in both hands, her teeth never parting as she spoke. "Turn it off now."

I arched a brow. "Make me."

The witch had the audacity to swing. Her actions caught me off-guard, and I didn't step out of the way in time. The razor-sharp edge nicked my arm, making blood pool in the shallow wound.

Astonishment and irritation mixed with a strange feeling of admiration. I could have forced her to turn on her friends in that instant, yet she straightened her spine and held her head high as if she actually thought she could vanquish me.

"Is that all you've got?" I teased.

"Enough." Chaos laid a hand on my shoulder. "Save it for the fae."

I wiped the blood from my arm and flicked a drop toward her before reeling in my magic.

"After swallowing roach goo, I'm not afraid of a little demon blood." She stood at the ready, her muscles flexed, her stance wide.

"You should be." I crossed my arms, the wound already healing. "It can drive people insane."

She flicked her gaze to Chaos, who said, "It's true."

"Fabulous." She rolled her eyes and shifted her attention to the body.

The woman had been disemboweled. A jagged, vertical cut from her neck to her pubic bone allowed her intestines to spill onto the pavement. Her lifeless eyes stared into the cloudy sky, and her mouth was frozen in a soundless scream.

"Anyone sense a rift?" Ember rose and glanced at me before focusing on my brother.

"I do not," he said.

"Neither do I. Not in the vicinity, anyway." I paused, an unmistakable energy registering in my psyche. The vibration pulled me north, and I strode toward it, my gaze bouncing over the scene, though vision would do no good for battling this vile creature.

"Where do you think you're going?" Ember shouted after me.

I turned around to find the witches backing away while several human workers examined the body. "To find the one responsible and end him."

"Not without us." Ember gestured for the others to follow, and she jogged to catch up. "What do you sense? Is it a demon after all?"

"It is not." I continued my trek, following the energy down an alley. A translucent mosaic pattern rippled in the air ahead of me, and I stopped, opening my senses even more and inhaling the rancid stench of fae.

"Is that what I think it is?" Chaos stopped beside me.

"Indeed it is." I cracked my knuckles, a smile lifting my lips. "A worthy adversary straight out of the gate. I believe I'm going to like it here."

The ripple shifted, and high-pitched chittering rang in my ears.

"Would you like to fill us in?" Ember stood on my other side, unafraid, though if she knew what lay in the alley ahead, she would have run and hidden.

"It's a fae foot soldier," Chaos said. "One rung above scouts."

"Where?" Shade asked.

"Look for the ripples in the air." Chaos pointed, and the fae moved across the alley. "They have cloaking powers, as do the upper fae horde."

"Fabulous. Now we're in the middle of a *Predator* movie." Ember held her hand toward Ash, who poured a blue substance into her palm. She hurled the granules at the fae, and they bounced off its body.

"Well, frack. That didn't work."

"It's part of their biology, not their magic." I gathered hellfire in my palm. "You can't counter it with a spell."

I hurled a fireball at the fae, and it screeched, scurrying up the wall. Its shroud failed for less than a second as it recovered, revealing two sets of human-like arms with taloned hands, large, faceted eyes, translucent wings, and pinchers protruding from each side of its mouth.

Ember sucked in a breath. "Oh, for Hecate's sake. Why do they all have to look like bugs?" Gripping her sword in both hands, she activated her fire magic, flames licking up the blade.

The fae's shroud returned, and it lunged, knocking Shade to the ground. His shadow magic rolled into him, bringing the world into full color, and he shot to his feet, clutching a wounded arm. "The asshole bit me."

Blood oozed from two puncture wounds on his biceps. "Are these venomous too?"

"From scouts up, they all are," Chaos said. "And they become more toxic the greater the fae."

"Guess we better mix a ton of antidotes when we get home." Ash pulled a bottle from her bag. "Hide from sight our magical plight. With the power of Shade, my intent is conveyed."

The world turned to grayscale again, and she clutched his good arm, dragging him to the alley entrance. He stiffened, the poison paralyzing him in seconds, and he collapsed to the ground.

Miles gathered energy between his palms. His efforts resulted in a baseball-sized sphere of electricity, and he threw it at the mosaic ripple. The fae darted out of the way before shimmying up the wall and leaping onto his chest, knocking him onto the pavement.

Ember swung her fiery blade, hitting the fae, and it leaped onto the wall, uninjured. She helped Miles stand and dashed toward her sister, returning with a plastic bottle. The fae rippled to her left, and she spun, hurling a fine white powder into the air. What spell she cast, I did not know. The fae dashed away before the powder reached it.

"What was that magic supposed to accomplish?" I asked.

"It's not magic; it's baby powder, and it clings to everything. If I could see the bastard, I could kill it." She searched the alley, squinting as if narrowing her vision would bring the pest into focus. "Why are you here? What do you want?"

"This is our world now," a gravelly, seemingly disembodied voice replied.

"The hell it is." She threw another mist of powder in the direction of the voice, but it missed its mark.

"Hell is next," he said.

Ember flew backward, slamming into a brick wall. She grunted and squeezed the bottle, coating the fae's head and torso in white powder.

Its pinchers opened and closed two inches from her face. "Witches will submit or die."

"I'll take option C." She reached down, retrieving a knife from a thigh holster, but the fae had armored exoskeletons. She was about to learn how useless her blades would be when my brother barreled into the pest, dragging it to the ground and punching it in the face.

Its pinchers caught his wrist, and as he pulled free, they sliced into his skin, leaving a deep, jagged cut on his arm. Chaos stood, stumbling backward, the venom already taking hold. Ash and Miles grabbed his arms, leading him to the alley exit and lowering him next to Shade.

Ember threw a dagger, lodging it in the fae's neck. It screeched, spinning and flailing as it grasped the handle and pulled it out.

"Demon blood should not affect me." It spit and wiped Chaos's blood from its pinchers. "How?"

"These aren't just any demons." Ember thrust her flame-licked sword beneath an armored plate, slicing into the fae. "They're Princes of Hell."

It coughed, its bug eyes moving in different directions, and green fae blood oozed from its mouth. Ember removed her sword, and with an elegant, ethereal spin, she swung, chopping off the creature's head.

I stood there, stunned, my mouth agape as the beast collapsed to the ground. She brushed past me, rushing to the others and checking their wounds. She offered Chaos a bandage before helping Shade to his feet, and a feeling of both admiration and awe warmed my chest.

Ember was no ordinary witch. She was a warrior. A leader.

A goddess to rival Athena herself.

"We need one more shadow spell so we can get rid of the body," she said.

Shade nodded. "I think I'm okay now."

"No." She touched his shoulder. "You need to recharge. I'll cast the bottled one."

Ash tossed her a glass container, and she removed the cork, reciting the same words her sister had used.

The world around us returned to gray. I had been so enamored watching her fight, I hadn't noticed when our surroundings shifted to color.

My brother and the women approached the body while the men returned their supplies to the bag Ash had carried. Chaos shot a stream of hellfire at the fae's severed head, turning it to ash.

"I can cut him into pieces if we need to," Ember said. "His exoskeleton looks as strong as the scout's."

"I believe the four of us can penetrate his armor." Chaos looked at me, and the witches followed his gaze.

Ember scoffed. "You mean the big, bad demon prince, whose favorite pastime is supposedly killing fae, is actually going to help now?"

Her goading broke me from my stupor. "I rather enjoyed watching you struggle. Perhaps I've found a new favorite pastime." In truth, it was not the struggle I enjoyed. It was her ingenuity, the way she commanded the situation...how stunning she looked while battling a foe who could kill a normal witch before they had the chance to utter a single spell.

Her jaw ticked. "Let's get this over with before the cloak wears off."

Ember lifted her hands, palms toward the dead fae, and released a stream of flames. Chaos and Ash followed suit, the exoskeleton flaking beneath their heat. I joined them, and the four of us worked together to burn through the overgrown insect's armor.

Slowly, slowly, the fae began to crumble. Five

minutes passed. Six. Seven, and finally, the creature turned into a pile of ashes.

Ember heaved a breath and leaned against the wall, wiping her forehead with the back of her hand. "That was fun."

I couldn't tell if she used sarcasm, but I had to agree. Watching her fight a worthy adversary had been thrilling.

Miles approached with Shade and handed the bag to Ash. "I guess we know what happened to the woman."

"Maybe." Ember retrieved her knife from the ground and sheathed her sword. "But humans are capable of much more violence than that, so we can't rule anything out."

"Did anyone get a close enough look at the body to see if all her organs were in place?" I asked.

"It'll take an autopsy to figure that out," Ash said. "Why?"

"If the woman is missing her liver," I said, "the fae was responsible for her demise."

Ember dragged a hand down her face. "Giant bugs who eat liver. My worst effing nightmare."

The fact this witch had entranced me with her battle skills was mine...

CHAPTER 11
EMBER

"You have to let us do this, or the entire coven will know what you are." I fisted my hand around the powdered potion Ash had mixed. After we'd cremated the fae soldier, we'd returned home and taken a moment to brush our teeth and change. Shade and Miles had stopped to get clean clothes, and the rest of us gathered in the kitchen.

"It's painless." Chaos sat on the stool next to Mayhem and rested his forearms on the counter. "You won't feel any different."

Mayhem scoffed. "I'm not afraid of pain, but I will not allow you to destroy my demonic nature. I *am* a demon. You can't change that."

I closed my eyes and tried not to grind my teeth. If I ever got the chance to see a dentist again, he'd probably pass out when he saw the nubs I had left. "We aren't trying to change you, though Hecate knows if we could take that ego down a notch or two, we would."

Mayhem narrowed his eyes. "You speak as though you aren't afraid of me in the slightest."

I held his gaze. "I think we've established that I'm not."

His expression shifted, one brow lifting, drawing up the corner of his mouth. "You should be. I could do things to you that you've never dared imagine."

A warm shiver formed at the base of my neck before heat spread through my body. I could imagine... *had* imagined plenty since my eyes first locked on his unwrapped package.

But nope. I was not going there. No way.

I lifted one shoulder dismissively. "Doubtful."

"Try me." His gaze smoldered, so I rolled my eyes and looked at his brother before my panties got wet.

Chaos drummed his fingers on the counter. "Cast the spell on me so he can see it's harmless. Surely the one you placed on me weeks ago has lost its potency."

"That's a good idea." Ash took my free hand. "We're used to him now, so it could be wearing off without us noticing."

I shook my head. "Do you remember how much vim it took to cast it last time? I'm not sure we can do it twice in a row."

"Last time we did it, Chrys's suppression spell was

active on the house," Ash said. "We're operating at full power now."

"A High Priestess who isn't strong enough to cast a spell twice." Mayhem chuckled. "Why am I not surprised?"

Whatever heat had built in my body from his smolder turned to ice. "Let's do it, and then I want the biggest, fattest breakfast burrito we can find."

Ash opened her vim to me, her magic flowing from her hand and into mine. I did the same, letting our powers mix and meld, bringing it all to the surface. "Aura strong, magic deep, we hide your essence from all who seek," we said in unison before blowing the fine pink powder toward Chaos.

"As we will it, so mote it be." My breath came out in a rush, and I tugged from my sister's grasp, splaying my fingers and fisting my hands three times while the fire magic coursing through my veins cooled to a simmer. Ash was right. With Chrys's stupid hex lifted from the house, I'd have no problem casting the spell again.

"I feel no different." Chaos held up his hand and ignited a ball of hellfire in his palm. "My powers are intact."

"Hmm..." Mayhem eyed his brother and shrugged.

"If you ever want to leave this house again, you need to demon up and let us do this." I tossed two bay leaves into a copper bowl. "Or are you afraid?"

His gaze snapped to mine, the intensity in his eyes almost making me regret goading him before his lips twitched as if he were suppressing amusement.

Ash crushed the lady's mantle, marjoram, and wolfsbane and dropped it into the bowl along with the liquid mix she'd concocted. I added the final ingredient—a single drop of cinnamon oil—and the potion sizzled and popped before turning to powder.

With the mixture complete, Mayhem inclined his chin. "Very well. I will play along with your game for now."

I glanced at my sword hanging on the wall. "It's your only choice, buddy."

He chuckled, this time not bothering to hide it, but at least he didn't argue.

Ash took my hand, and we recited the incantation again, blowing the powder into Mayhem's face this time.

He stiffened, his brow furrowing in confusion. "Are you certain it worked?"

"It worked." I returned the herbs to the cabinet while Ash washed the dishes. The second time we cast the spell, I did feel the tax on my vim, though it wasn't nearly bad enough to warrant the three-hour nap I'd have liked to take.

Mayhem summoned hellfire into his palm, turning his hand over and letting the ball of burning light roll across the back of his hand before he extinguished it.

Seemingly satisfied his powers remained intact, he nodded and looked at me. "Tell me about these breakfast burritos."

"They're divine. Let's go."

AFTER WALKING THREE UNEVENTFUL BLOCKS—THANK you, Hecate—we chowed down on chorizo and egg burritos, drank way too much coffee, and returned to Ash's studio, where Shade and Miles were waiting.

She poured the salt circle and lit the candles at each point of the pentagram before taking a piece of chalk from a drawer and holding it up. "Who wants to do Discord's sigil?"

"I will." I grabbed the chalk from her hand before one of the guys volunteered. Not that I didn't have faith in their artistic abilities, especially Miles's. He was a great artist, but Ash felt like it was cheating or something for her to draw another demon's mark. Chaos was *Ash's demon.* I had to make damn sure Mayhem didn't become mine.

"Hold on. You need to see this." Miles gestured for us to watch a video on his phone.

Chief Higgins stood behind a podium, the Salem police emblem, four feet in diameter, hanging on the wall behind him. An American flag hung from a pole to his right, and four microphones of different shapes sat on the stand in front of him.

"The woman who was murdered this morning is believed to be the third victim." His expression was somber, but a spark of anger tightened his eyes. "The manner of death is identical with all three, and they happened within the span of two days."

"Shit. Turn it up." This was bad. Very, very bad.

"If anyone has information, we encourage you to contact the police department non-emergency line as quickly as possible. Until the culprits have been captured, we will be enforcing an eight PM to sunrise curfew within the city limits. Stay vigilant, folks, and lock your doors."

I stretched my neck. "So the disgusting flyman killed three people before we took him out."

"Or there's more than one," Ash said. "We never found the rift he got through."

Miles returned his phone to his pocket. "Or there's a serial killer on the loose. We need to know if their livers were missing."

"On it." I dialed Higgins's cell and put it on speaker.

He picked up on the second ring. "Don't tell me..."

"Had their livers been taken?" I asked.

He missed a beat before he replied. "Yes. What kind of monster are we dealing with?"

"It's a fae from across the veil," Shade said. "We killed it this morning."

"You could have told me that before I called a press

conference." Annoyance dripped from his voice, as usual. "Now I have my men on the hunt for a serial killer."

"You could have called me when you found the first victim." I matched his tone.

"It looked mundane." He blew out a hard breath. "I hate to say this, but has anyone in your coven considered joining the force? You could be a paid consultant."

Now there was an idea… "Maybe when all this is through. Keep your team on the hunt and call me if anyone else gets killed."

"I thought you said you took the perp out," he said.

"We did, but there could be more soon. A lot more."

"Great." He hung up the phone, and I shoved mine into my back pocket.

I made a grabby motion to Ash, and she handed me her phone with Discord's sigil on the screen. Dropping to my knees, I laid it in the circle and pressed the chalk to the floor.

"He'll owe you nothing," Mayhem said.

I glanced over my shoulder to find him staring at my butt. Typical. "That's why you're here. Convince him like Chaos did you."

I returned to my canvas, dragging the chalk downward before looping up and creating a sharp ninety-degree angle. The phone pinged, and a message from Patrice slid across the screen. I finished the sigil and rose, handing it to Ash. "It's Patrice asking if we've summoned Discord yet."

Ash typed on her screen. A moment later, it pinged again. "She says she's not comfortable being in the house with the demons." She shrugged and laid her phone on the table.

"As long as she keeps her mouth shut about the source of this fiasco, I don't care. We'll go to her if we need healing." I held out my hands, and Shade and Chaos took them. Ash stood between her demon and Miles. "Everyone remember the incantation?"

Mayhem strolled toward Miles, reaching for his hand.

"Not you." I pinned the unruly demon with a hard glare. "Just stand in the corner like a good boy."

He arched a brow. "You allow Chaos to participate. Why not me?"

"I trust him." I couldn't believe I uttered those words aloud, but there I was, admitting I trusted a demon. He might have been a pain in my ass at times, but with the way he treated my sister, I couldn't deny it. This Prince of Hell had no ill intent toward us. And he loved Ash beyond belief.

Mayhem crossed his arms. "Are you sure that's a wise decision? A witch trusting a demon?"

"It is what it is. Now hush so we can finish this."

Ash swallowed hard and nodded, and pain tightened my chest. How awful it must have been knowing her relationship with the love of her life had an expiration date and she...we...were helping to bring it on sooner.

Chaos opened himself, letting his magic run from his hand into mine. It tingled, filling me with a power that could be addictive if I wasn't careful. I let it flow into Shade, and he gasped before letting out a slow, satisfied breath.

Very addictive.

We recited the words like demon-summoning pros —which it looked like we were becoming—our magic mixing and melding, the energy in the room thickening like boiling water with flour. The weight of Mayhem's gaze on me was palpable, but I didn't dare look at him. Latin was tricky. If I pronounced one syllable wrong, the entire spell could explode. On the final word, we focused our energy on the salt circle, activating the containment ring.

"Not bad," Mayhem said, though he didn't sound the slightest bit impressed. "But my former host could have created one just as strong on her own."

My mouth tightened, and I did my best not to grind my teeth. He was baiting me. I knew he was, but I couldn't help myself. "Your former host..."

My mind blanked. I'd hoped for a barbed, snarky comeback, but he was right. Chrys could make a circle just as strong. She *had* on several occasions. Could I have made one strong enough to hold a demon prince?

According to Chaos, not with the spell I'd used before. But this one was different. It wasn't dark magic, but it hovered in the gray area, for sure.

And I certainly wasn't going to take chances by going solo just to impress this infuriating asshat.

He smirked. "Are you planning to finish that sentence this decade?"

"No. No, I'm not." I strode to the table and opened the grimoire to the summoning spell before scanning the words. "Let's bring in Discord and finish this."

"What are you offering him?" Mayhem walked toward me with a cocky gait and glanced at the summoning spell.

"A chance to right a wrong." I turned the grimoire toward Shade, and he and Miles studied the spell.

Mayhem laughed. "If the curse on your bloodline is the wrong to which you're referring, you will be sorely disappointed. Isabel is the one who wronged you. We simply did as she requested in exchange for her soul."

I crossed my arms. "Which you never got to claim because she outsmarted you."

Ash touched her fingers to my elbow, her silent reminder to cool my jets. We had more important things to do than to waste time one-upping an arrogant hellion.

"Everyone ready?" I closed the book.

"Good luck convincing him to pass through

without an offering," he said. "We came easily because you released us from prison. Discord is already free."

"What did Isabel offer when she summoned you?" Ash asked Chaos.

"Her soul," Shade answered for him. "He already said that."

"We will entice Discord with the chance to claim our prize." Chaos moved next to his brother, laying a palm on his shoulder. "For Isabel's debt finally to be paid."

"Revenge." Mayhem nodded. "It might work."

"It's worth a shot. Shall we?" Ash held out her hand, and Chaos took it. "Someone hold on to Mayhem. If Discord senses his brothers here, he's more likely to come through."

"And bring Cinder with him?" Miles took Ash's other hand.

"If she is alive," Mayhem said.

"She is. Come on." I grabbed Mayhem's hand, and pinpricks spiraled up my arm to lodge in my chest. I grasped Chaos with my other hand, but he didn't affect me like Mayhem. He never had.

And those pinpricks coming from the latest addition to our demon collection...? Not *un*pleasant in the slightest. He felt like raw power, and my body wanted more.

Shade strolled around the circle to take Mayhem's free hand, and I watched him for a sign that the pinpricks registered in his psyche like they did mine. He didn't react, but I had no doubt once the demon shared his energy with us, then Shade would feel it. How could he not?

"Ready, set, go." I let my magic run down my arms and into the demons on either side of me. Okay, yes... I did send a smidge more power into Mayhem, just to remind him I wasn't some dainty little kitchen witch. He might've been a hurricane, but I was no light afternoon rain.

He cut his gaze toward me, one corner of his mouth lifting either in amusement or appreciation. I didn't dare ask which.

Chaos opened to me first, the familiar tingles of Underworld magic seeping into my palm and filling my body with power. I allowed it to flow into Mayhem, and he chuckled.

"Are you holding back, brother?"

Chaos's fingers twitched. "As should you. Witches are mortal beings."

Shade gasped and swallowed hard, and Mayhem laughed again. The pinpricks buzzing through my body intensified before a tidal wave of untamed magic blasted through my psyche, setting my nerves ablaze.

I did my best not to react, but damn. This demon made every part of my body tingle.

Every. Part.

I cleared my throat to stop my voice from coming out as a squeak. "All of us together."

We recited the summoning spell in unison. Nothing happened.

I squeezed the guys' hands. "Again, and this time give it everything you've got."

The demon magic running through me intensified, and we spoke the words three more times. Still nothing.

"I told you that you needed an offering." Mayhem tried to pull from my grasp, but I tightened my grip. "Share more of your power. We need to make damn sure Discord knows his brothers are here."

A raging river of strong, feral electricity flowed into me, spiraling through my body and making my toes curl in my boots. I fought a gasp, again not daring to let him know how he affected me. I refused to give him the satisfaction.

We performed the summoning a fifth time, a sixth, and light flickered inside the circle. A stream of dark green smoke poured into the ring, the impression of a featureless face forming in the fog, reminding me of the scene in *The Mummy* when Imhotep's face formed in the sandstorm...creepy AF. It moved around the perimeter, pausing first on Chaos and then Mayhem.

"Have you the amulet?" Discord's voice echoed, sounding a million miles away.

"We have the means to avenge our imprisonment,"

Chaos said. "Join us in the mortal realm so we can identify Isabel's descendants and claim our prize."

"I owed a debt to the witch who freed me, and no one else." Something about the way he said it raised the hairs on the back of my neck... Past tense. Whatever Cinder had asked for, he'd already done it.

And she hadn't come back.

"That's our sister, Cinder," Ash said. "She needs you to find our parents and bring them all here to break my family's curse."

His distant, ominous laugh sounded like it came from the deepest depths of Hell...which it did. "That was not the debt she asked I pay."

Mayhem dropped my hand and stepped toward the circle. "Join us, brother. We have fae to battle."

"Find my amulet, and I will consider it." In a flash of light and a thunderous boom, the smoke dissipated, taking the demon to his own side of the veil.

"What the actual eff?" Ash looked at me with a furrowed brow. "In the journal, that's exactly what she said she would ask for."

I swallowed hard, the blood draining from my head to my feet as the realization sank in. "It was..."

"Too much to ask," Mayhem said matter-of-factly.

"Too many requests," Chaos added. At least he had the peopling skills to sound worried for us.

"But she freed him from four hundred years of imprisonment." Ash's mouth hung open as she looked from me to the demons. "How is that too much to ask?"

I ticked the list off on my fingers. "Take her to Hell, find our parents, save them from the demon who took them, bring all three of them back to this realm, break the family curse…and not kill any of us along the way."

Ash covered her mouth, shaking her head before lifting her hand and dropping it at her side. "All she asked for in return for his release was a ticket to Hell."

I nodded. "Because she thought she could do all the rest by herself." Which was typical of Cinder. Our eldest sister excelled at everything…except asking for help.

Ash extinguished the candles and carried them to the storage cabinet. "We need a new plan."

"We need to go to Hell ourselves and bring her back." I swiped my foot through the salt to break the containment circle. Really, I just wanted to kick something, but whatever.

Chaos's expression was so grim, I didn't need an interpretation. "I'm afraid that isn't possible. Your sister is lost."

CHAPTER 12
MAYHEM

"This doesn't make sense. Why can't we go to Hell and get her?" Ember paced the length of the library before turning on her heel and returning to the desk where her sister sat.

Ash's fingers flew across the keys of her computer… a device they swore contained no magic, yet it had the power to access the knowledge of this realm as if tapping into the Akashic Records.

"And he won't bring her back because we don't have some necklace he lost eons ago?" Ember waved her hands in the air, clearly having a fit of hysterics.

I leaned toward Chaos. "Are you affecting her brain?"

"He wouldn't dare," Ash said, her eyes never straying from the screen.

I looked to my brother for confirmation, and he

shook his head. He had been tamed...whipped...by a witch. How pathetic. Although...

I let my gaze wander over Ember's form. I wouldn't mind her attempts to tame me if it meant I could ravish her every night as she tried. Perhaps I should challenge her to a wrestling match so she could work out her hysteria...naked, of course.

"What does this artifact even do? Why does he want it so bad? We were this close." She held her thumb and forefinger half an inch apart before turning and pacing again.

I moved to block her path, taking her shoulders in my hands. "Calm down, woman. Sit, and I will answer your questions."

"Oh, boy," Ash said under her breath, and my brother chuckled.

A vein pulsed in Ember's neck, and her lips flattened, a wildness I hadn't yet seen swirling in her eyes. Her jaw moved from side to side as she held my gaze, silently challenging me, a Prince of Hell. She was either unafraid or unaware of the fact I could snap her neck with a twist of my wrist.

Slowly, she lowered her gaze to my right hand on her shoulder. Flicking back to my eyes, she arched a brow, still not saying a word. Her fingers curled into fists at her sides, and she cocked her head. "Get. Your. Hands. Off me."

As if by instinct, I jerked from her shoulders,

releasing her. How odd. My normal reaction to a demand like that would have been to grip her tighter.

She brushed past me and returned to the desk. "I guess you didn't think to have *that* conversation with him while you binged reality TV?"

"I did not." Chaos lowered his eyes before looking at me. "Telling a woman of this century to calm down will have the opposite effect of what you hope to achieve. It's a lesson I learned the hard way." He gently squeezed his witch's shoulders.

She patted his hand. "Lucky for him, he's a fast learner."

"To answer your first question, Ember..." Chaos sat on the edge of the desk. "We cannot take you both to Hell because if four beings of such power as ours were to pass through the veil at the same time, it would collapse."

"You don't know that for sure." She crossed her arms, jutting out one hip and tapping her foot. "I say we try it and see."

"I agree," I said. "It's the only way to know for certain." And the idea of watching her do battle in my realm made my dick twitch.

"Hold on." Ash held a palm toward us. "Let's explore your leap-first look-later method."

Ember rolled her eyes. "Then it becomes a plan."

"Which is my specialty." Ash smirked. "Say we do

make it across without collapsing the veil. How would we return without someone to summon us?"

"What are we? Incompetent slugs? We'll bring you back." Shade's voice drew my attention to the two men in the corner. I had forgotten they played a role in this game.

Ember gestured to them grandly. "Problem solved."

"Not quite." Ash swiveled her chair toward us and folded her hands in her lap. "Think about it. The biggest issues with the veil started when Cinder summoned Discord, right?"

"Obviously." She continued pacing.

"So the main damage occurred when Discord came through, and then they both crossed over." She opened a large book and traced her finger down the page containing our marks before tapping it. "Read this." She turned the volume toward her sister.

Ember stopped and examined the page. "'Discord, Chaos, and Mayhem are the original Princes of Hell, created by the Lord of the Underworld himself. Their strength and power are unmatched, and all of demonkind obey them.' What is this? An ego-stroking session? They're demon royalty. We know."

"Not that. Read the section titled 'Warnings.'"

She sniffed and looked at the passage again. "'Summoning an entity of this power will weaken the veil between worlds. You must keep the demon contained for a period of one week before sending him back to his realm. Doing so too soon may cause… irreparable damage.' Well, damn."

She inhaled, opening her mouth to say more, but my brother cut her off. "With my summoning, the veil only weakened marginally."

Ash nodded. "It's worse since I brought Chaos over, but the damage didn't double. Same with Mayhem."

Ember crossed her arms, drumming her fingers against her biceps. "When Chrys brought him over, you vanquished him right away. That didn't cause irreparable damage."

"Because he didn't have a corporeal form," Shade said. "Now he does."

"I haven't sensed a rift today, and we have been out in the city twice. Let's keep it that way." Chaos rose to his feet. "*If* someone is to cross over to the Underworld, we must wait at least a week."

"Waiting is not my thing. I need to battle another beastie ASAP." She rested a hand on her hip, drawing my gaze to the curve of her waist. How could a warrior of her magnitude possess such delicate features?

"What's the amulet he wants?" Miles asked. "Maybe if we can find it, no one will have to go to the Underworld."

"It was a gift from Lucifer." My lip curled. Discord was the first Prince of Hell and had always been the

King's favorite. Lucifer allowed him into the most private parts of the palace, making him privy to the inner workings and plans of our realm. He was the Lord of the Underworld's pet.

Chaos chuckled. "It wasn't a gift. Discord won it in a bet."

I frowned. "He told me it was a gift."

"Because the bet was about whether or not you could beat Cerberus in a wrestling match when they were a puppy." He laughed again. "They were half your size, and they took you down in sixty seconds, sitting on your stomach and nibbling on your pants with all three of their mouths while you bellowed about it not being a fair fight."

"Oof." Ash scrunched her face, and Ember rolled her lips inward, holding back a laugh.

Cold flashed in my chest before hellfire rose from my gut, spreading through my body and making my ears burn. It *hadn't* been a fair fight, and Chaos knew it. Yet there he was, ridiculing me in front of this coven.

I should not have cared. I was the third Prince, the afterthought. My brothers having fun at my expense was nothing new, but the fact that these four witches...that Ember...now knew of their mockery made my stomach roil and my skin crawl.

Unable to meet her gaze, I turned toward the bookshelves and examined the mess they called a library. Ancient grimoires lay haphazardly on the floor, and dust coated the empty spaces on the shelves where the books should have been.

"What does the amulet do?" Ember asked, her hysteria under control, but I couldn't answer.

My blood began to boil, anger flushing out the shame my brother had caused. How dare he attempt to humiliate me, to say to these witches that I was less than his equal. That I couldn't best a *puppy*. It was time to prove what Mayhem could do.

I focused on Shade, sending my mind magic into his psyche. His eyes widened. Then they narrowed. He glared at my brother, cracking his knuckles before taking a blade from his holster. With a guttural roar, he charged toward Chaos, plunging the knife into my brother's neck.

Chaos turned, swinging his arm and knocking the witch backward. Shade careened into the wall, cracking the sheetrock, but my magic was stronger than any injury he might have sustained. The witch lunged again. Chaos caught him by the throat and lifted him from the ground.

"Brother..." He said, his tone scolding.

I focused on Miles, sending him the same pulse of magic I had given Shade. He fisted his hands and blew out a hard breath like a bull ready to charge.

I felt the tip of the blade on my chest before I noticed Ember had drawn her sword. She stood in front of me, her eyes narrowed, her head slightly cocked. "What did I tell you about being a good boy?"

"Boy?" I growled low in my throat. "I am more man than you could handle."

She pressed her blade harder against my chest. "Release them. Now."

Miles gathered energy between his palms as he glared at my brother. With his free hand, Chaos removed the knife from his neck. Shade, who had been thrashing in his grip, now hung limp.

"Please, Mayhem." Ash moved next to her sister. "We can't do this without you. We need to work together."

I cut my gaze from her to Miles. He lifted his hands, preparing to throw his magic.

"Alright then. Back to Hell you go." Ember gripped her sword with both hands. Had the blade not been precisely over my heart, I would have let her stab me.

But I had no intention of returning to Hell now. Not when I had havoc to spread through Salem.

I released my hold on the men. Miles gasped, looking at the energy in his hands as if he couldn't recall summoning it. He made fists, extinguishing the power, and Chaos dropped Shade on the floor.

The witch coughed before sucking in a large breath and rubbing his neck. "What the hell was that?"

"That was Mayhem attempting to prove a point."

Chaos rubbed the puncture on his neck, his fingers bloody from the wound.

"Which he won't do again. You are not to mess with any coven member's mind. Ever." Ember twisted the blade, reminding me she would take no issue in vanquishing me should I not behave to her standards.

How far would I have to go for her to act on her word? Perhaps I would find out before this was through.

"Your powers are different. Chaos causes confusion and panic that sometimes turns into fights." She sheathed her sword. "You go straight to violence."

"We are not the same, if that's what you're implying," I said. "Much like you are the brawn while Ash has the brains."

She nodded her head, shrugging one shoulder at my insult. "That's fair."

"She's smarter than you think," Ash said, defending her sister's intelligence. I doubted Ember needed defense from anyone, though. I'd never met a woman so fierce.

Shade rose to his feet. "Do that again, and I'll suck the life out of you so slowly, you'll beg me to vanquish you."

I lit a small ball of fire and let it roll over and under each of my fingers before I extinguished it in my palm. "I would like to see you try, shadow witch. I won't be tamed like my brother."

Shade puffed out his chest, but Miles rested a hand on his shoulder, calming him.

Ember crossed her arms. "Check your egos, boys. We're on the same team."

I arched a brow. "Are we?"

Her mouth tightened. "We're pretending like we are. Now, what does the amulet do, and why won't Discord accept our summons without it?"

CHAPTER 13
EMBER

"There's nothing in the book about it, and I couldn't find anything on the witchy web." Ash turned to the index of the stolen volume and searched again, but if she couldn't find it the first time, it wasn't there. Ash was a research master.

"It would have no documentation." Mayhem strolled toward the staircase and headed up without another word.

Silence hung over us for a beat or two before Ash hit Chaos's arm with the back of her hand. "You embarrassed him. Go apologize."

The demon shrugged. "I spoke the truth. It was time he knew."

"He's embarrassed," Ash said again.

"Embarrassment and shame are two emotions my

brother is incapable of feeling." He took a tissue from Ash's desk and cleaned the blood from his fingers and neck. The wound was already healing.

"I'm siding with Chaos on this one. He's pissed for sure, but embarrassed? That guy?" I laughed. "Come on. Let's head up."

I ascended the stairs and found Mayhem in the kitchen, shoveling chocolate chips into his mouth. What was it with demons and sugar?

He swallowed and filled his hand with more. "The amulet increases power. Whatever magic the being possesses will multiply when they wear it."

I tilted my head, an idea wriggling in the back of my mind as the others joined us. "What else?"

He shoved the handful of chocolate into his mouth. "It's the only reason Discord is the most powerful of princes. Without it, he's no stronger than Chaos or me."

"Isabel must have taken it before she imprisoned him." Chaos held out his hand, and Mayhem begrudgingly filled it with chocolate. "Lucifer made him swear never to take it off, especially in this realm. It's too powerful for a mortal to bear."

"And he won't come back to earth unless he can be stronger than his brothers?" Shade sank onto a stool. "He sounds like a pompous prick."

"Takes one to know one," Ash said with a grin.

"Ha ha." Shade rolled his eyes and laughed.

I would never get used to their new dynamic. A month ago, they'd be close to strangling each other by now. A month ago, everything was different. Everything...

The wriggling idea burrowed deep in my brain, dissolving all traces of doubt. "I know where the amulet is." Of course I did. It made so much sense, any other explanation sounded ridiculous.

"Care to share?" Ash grabbed a box of crackers from the pantry and sat next to Shade.

"Isn't it obvious?" I met each of their expectant gazes, but no one had a clue. "Chrys had it. How else could she have gotten so strong so quickly?"

Ash stopped chewing, her brow furrowing as the gears turned in her mind. "But...how did she find it? If Isabel had it, wouldn't it have been hidden...? And how would Chrys even know it existed?"

"She must be Isabel's descendant." Miles took a beer from the fridge and sat at the table.

"That makes sense." Shade joined him. "She said she had no choice. When Cinder confided in her about her plans to summon Discord, Chrys did as Isabel had instructed and tried to free the others so she could beg for forgiveness."

I grabbed a beer and paced the length of the kitchen. "And the whole Boston ordeal was her trying to claim what was hers by birthright. Isabel was the High Priestess of Boston in her time."

"Wait." Miles picked at the label on his bottle. "If Isabel was High Priestess, isn't their current leader a descendant?"

"No," Ash said around a mouthful of crackers before she swallowed. "Their leadership changed families around three hundred years ago. I couldn't find the reason in my research, but her descendants haven't been in charge for centuries."

Mayhem dropped the empty chocolate chip bag on the counter and wiped the corners of his mouth with his fingers.

"The trash can is over there." Ash pointed, giving him *the look,* as if she could command him the way she did Chaos.

He ignored her. "Chrys is not Isabel's descendant."

Ash's eye twitched, so I grabbed the bag and threw it away. "How do you know that? Chaos said it would take all three of you together to identify her bloodline."

He took a beer from the fridge and drank a long, slow pull. "You forget I spent time inside her, melding with her power. I am certain she is not a descendant."

"She could be." I took a swig, the icy bubbles cooling me on their way down. "She's so many generations removed, her blood was diluted with other families' magic. Maybe you missed it."

"I missed nothing but the chance to burn through her vessel and take her power as my own." He arched a brow accusingly, as if I would ever allow that to happen on my watch.

"I believe him," Chaos said. "When I was inside Ash, I recognized her bloodline as soon as she told me who she was."

"Did Chrys tell you who she was?" I sat on a stool by Ash.

"She told me nothing." He set his empty bottle on the counter.

"Recycle bin is blue." Ash cleared her throat, but he ignored her again. "Most likely, she's not a descendant, but we won't rule it out entirely. How she found the amulet...how she knew it existed...doesn't matter at this point. *Something* helped her gain all that power, and we need to find it."

"Guys!" I slapped my hand on the counter, making Ash jump. "You both said Chrys helped you grow your power. Did she use an artifact of any kind? Did you notice a different necklace or anything?"

Miles and Shade looked at each other, both scrunching their faces in concentration before Shade shook his head. "She didn't give me anything while we practiced except the knowledge of how to tap into power I already had. She was always wearing different jewelry. I don't pay attention to stuff like that."

He lifted his hands in an *I don't know* gesture. "I wasn't even aware she was training Miles or Ginger. She kept us separated and swore each of us to secrecy."

My shoulders slumped. "Miles?"

He shook his head. "If she had the amulet, she kept it hidden."

"Well, frack." My elbows thudded on the counter. "It wasn't on her when she died. I checked her pockets too."

"It could have fallen off in all the commotion," Ash said.

"If it's in the church basement, we'll never find it." I rested my chin on my fists. "That place looks like a tornado blew through it."

"I didn't sense its power while I resided inside her," Mayhem said. "If it were on her person, I would have felt it, and if she knew where the amulet came from...that it belonged to my brother...she would have hidden it before she summoned me if she were wise."

"So you don't have to be wearing it for it to increase your magic." Miles peeled off the label, closing his fist around it when Ash gave him the side eye.

"Perhaps not," Chaos said. "Discord, Lucifer, and Hecate know its full power. We know only what he told us."

"Hecate?" I straightened.

Mayhem nodded. "She and Lucifer forged it together, sharing their magic to create it."

"Well, then. Let's ask her where it is." I rose and went to the herb cabinet to gather supplies for our ritual. If they had led with that bit of information, we wouldn't have wasted the last half hour discussing theories. "Ash, get the candles and sage ready."

"On it." She opened the smudge drawer and gathered the dried herb, laying it on the counter before unrolling a length of twine.

Shade joined us in the kitchen. "Don't tell me you throw away your smudge sticks every time you use them."

Ash opened another drawer and gestured to the four bundles inside. "Of course we reuse them, but we're asking a goddess for help. She gets a new one. We'll use it to cleanse our space and make it ready for us to receive her guidance, and then we'll leave it as an offering."

He leaned a hip against the counter and crossed his arms. "You're not worried about forcing your demons out of the house?"

"Sage alone cannot physically repel us," Chaos said.

"But the odor is pungent enough to make us voluntarily leave." Mayhem wrinkled his nose and rose to his feet.

"Sit down. You're not going anywhere." I dropped crushed mugwort, a dash of wormwood, and some yarrow and mandrake into a copper bowl. "You two are as much a part of the family curse as we are. Hecate needs to see us working together."

I took the bowl to the living room and set it on the coffee table. Ash put black candles on either side, and I added two dog figurines to the altar.

"How can we help?" Miles asked.

"Oh, shit." Shade stared at his phone. "*Boston Live* released a story about a serial killer who has disemboweled his third victim in the city. Three there. Three here. That makes six total. It can't be the same fae we killed this morning."

"Livers removed?" I dragged the table away from the sofa so we could sit on the floor around it.

"It doesn't say." Miles gazed at Shade's phone over his shoulder. "Should we tell them what's going on?"

"No." I rubbed my forehead to chase away the headache threatening to form. "We got lucky when the Boston Magic Society blamed Chrys for the library incident. The less contact we have with them, the better."

Miles flashed an incredulous look. "But people are dying. If they knew about the fae, they could help."

Ash laughed dryly. "I doubt a bunch of dark witches will care about humans getting murdered. Let Boston deal with Boston."

"But they will care about a fae invasion and the potential collapse of the veil if it happens." Shade returned his phone to his pocket.

I tapped my finger against my lips as an idea formed in my mind. "Miles, do you still have the number of the woman you seduced? What was her name?"

He cringed. "Wendy. But I didn't seduce her."

"You just led her on and promised her a dinner date if she let you into the BMS library." I arranged the pillows on the couch, making our space more inviting for the goddess. "Totally not seductive. Do you have her number?"

His shoulders inched toward his ears. "Yeah..."

"Call her. Make good on your promise and arrange a dinner date. You'll find out what Boston knows and gently feed her information that she can report back."

"How diabolical." Mayhem grinned. "I like it."

Miles sighed. "I'll text her after the ritual."

I shook my head. "Do it now, and then you and Shade go patrol. The curse is a family affair. I don't want anyone else's energy clouding our intent."

Shade's brow slammed down. "It's our intent too. We all want to end this."

"Your Priestess is right," Mayhem said. "Hecate can be tricky. Her mystery eludes comprehension, but she is more likely to respond if the request comes only from those directly involved."

Shade let out a dry laugh. "You speak like you've actually met her."

Mayhem shrugged. "I have."

"As have I," Chaos added.

"Hmpf." Shade jerked his head toward the door.

"C'mon, Miles. Let's go kick some fae ass without them."

Miles followed him downstairs, and I gathered fire in my fingertip to light the sage.

Ash opened the window, and I smudged the room, fanning extra smoke into the four corners. "Negativity be gone. Only love and light may remain."

Yes, I might have fanned some in Mayhem's direction, but in my defense, he had a helluva negative attitude that grated on my last nerve. He coughed hard, narrowing his eyes at me. Chaos wrinkled his nose, his lips peeling back in disgust.

Neither of them moved from their seats, and I had to admit I was a little disappointed. It would have been fun to watch them get sucked out the window like the vampires in *True Blood* when Sookie rescinded their invitation.

Ash let out a tiny cough before closing the pane. "That's strong. I forgot how potent a new smudge stick can be."

I held her gaze, trying to keep my expression neutral. The smell wasn't strong at all.

"Let's do this thing." She plopped onto the floor, sitting cross-legged at the coffee table, and I extinguished the smudge stick before setting it by the bowl.

Chaos joined Ash on the floor, sitting next to her, which meant I had to sit by Mayhem. Ash smirked as we settled on the floor across from them, and I pursed my lips. My little sis read so many romance novels, I could only imagine what tropes she was applying to our situation. Forced proximity? Enemies to lovers? Thank the goddess we had more than one bed.

I laid my arm on the table, and Ash rested her hand in mine. The guys did the same, and I reluctantly...*very* reluctantly...slipped my other hand into Mayhem's. The same, not unpleasant, pin-pricking sensation danced across my palm before spiraling up my arm. He wasn't actively sharing his power, but something magical permeated his skin, spreading through my body and waking up nerves I never knew existed.

"Hecate prefers to call our king Hades, so it's best if that's how you refer to him during the ritual." Chaos's voice drew my attention away from the sensations in my body and back to the issue at hand.

I said a silent thank you to my sister's demon before tugging from Ash's grasp and lighting the candles. Staring at a flame, I allowed my vision to blur until everything in my periphery bled into nothingness. The fire flickered in response to our magic, stilling as we all cleared our minds and focused on our goddess.

"Everyone ready?" Ash asked.

We all murmured our agreement, and she lit the bowl of herbs ablaze before placing her palm in mine once more. "We call on the goddess Hecate," she said.

"Please accept our offering and show us a sign of your presence."

I opened my senses, searching the ether for a signal that the goddess had heard our request. All I felt was the low, prickling vibration of the demon sitting next to me. Funny... I couldn't recall feeling Chaos's energy this strongly, even when he'd held my hand.

"Hecate, please hear our words," I said. "We are desperate for your assistance."

"Do you feel her?" Ash asked.

"I don't." I looked at her, my vision swimming back into focus.

"She either didn't hear your plea, or she chose to ignore it." Mayhem kept a tight grip on my hand.

"Shoot." Ash tugged from my grasp and stood. "We forgot the crystals."

She padded to the shelf and grabbed a piece of black tourmaline and labradorite before setting them by the candles.

"Good choice." I laid my arm on the table and took her hand again.

"What do the crystals do?" Chaos asked.

"Black tourmaline is for protection and grounding," Ash said. "We need the grounding properties now, but we used its protection to get through the electrified doorway at the BMS library."

"I remember." He smiled, flashing her an endearing look.

"Labradorite enhances intuition and psychic abilities," I said. "It will help us sense her in the ether."

"Apparently, you don't perform this ritual often or you would not have forgotten such an essential part," Mayhem said, goading me yet again.

"Excuse me for having a lot on my already-overflowing plate. At least I didn't lose a wrestling match with a puppy." I fought the urge to stick out my tongue.

His teeth clicked. "Chaos slipped marrow from hellcat bones into my pocket before the match. Had I known, it would have ended differently."

I pressed my lips together. If I wasn't hyperfocused on connecting with Hecate, I'd have laughed. "Let's try again while the offering is still burning."

I stared at a flame again, allowing my vision to blur, opening myself to the ether once more. "We call on the goddess Hecate. Please accept our offering and show us a sign of your presence."

We waited, searching, focusing... Nothing.

"Chaos, you try," Ash said.

He recited the same words. Ash said them after him, but still I felt nothing.

"Your turn." I squeezed Mayhem's hand.

"If she ignored the three of you, I doubt she'll heed my call."

"Try," Ash and I said in unison.

He cleared his throat. "Hecate, please cast all animosity aside and hear the witches' plea."

Animosity? What history did he have with the goddess of witchcraft? I made a mental note to ask him later.

"Make your request," Chaos said. "She could be listening but prefers to keep her presence shrouded."

"It's worth a shot." I straightened my spine. "Goddess, as you must know, these demons cursed our bloodline centuries ago. They have agreed to help us break it and to restore the veil to its rightful state, but we need your help."

"You forged an amulet with Hades," Ash said. "One that Discord won in a bet. It's here, in our realm, and we need to find it. Please guide us on our quest. As we will it, so mote it be."

I stilled, focusing on nothing but the ether, seeing nothing but the flame, hearing nothing but my pulse in my ears. My body swayed, going deeper and deeper into the trance. I stayed there, waiting, feeling, listening.

Nothing. No answers. Not even a tiny clue.

With a deep inhale, I brought my senses back to the present and tugged from Ash's and Mayhem's grasps. "Well, that was a waste of time."

Ash's brow furrowed. "She's never ignored us before. Could it be because the guys are with us?"

Chaos stood. "We'll wait downstairs while you try it again."

Mayhem rose to his feet, and I gave him a pointed look. "Do not leave the building."

"I wouldn't dare." Amusement danced in his eyes as he lied.

When the demons left the room, I dumped the offering and refilled the bowl with fresh herbs before smudging the living room again. Ash sneezed four times before closing the window.

"I think I'm developing an allergy," she said.

"Maybe so." Or maybe her connection to Chaos was making her react to the herbs. Or worse...the curse was trying to take hold. Ash...the third-born Holland witch...would wipe out the entire coven if it came to fruition. Something inside her would have to fundamentally change for her to purposely hurt people. She was the kindest person I knew, but her reaction to the sage didn't bode well.

I lit the herbs as she sat across from me, and we made the offering again, pleading with the goddess to hear us, to help us.

"Anything?" I asked.

"Nothing," Ash replied.

"Damn." Fatigue washed over me, but it wasn't my body that was tired. It was my soul. If our goddess had abandoned us, how could we ever complete our quest and set things right?

I stood and returned the crystals and figurines to the shelf. "We could scry for it."

Ash took the bowl and candles to the kitchen. "We could, but I don't think I have enough vim left."

I rolled my neck. "I don't either, honestly. Not after how much we've used today."

She rinsed the bowl and dried it with a dishcloth. "We could also think rationally and look for it in the one place it most likely is."

"Good idea. And we can grab some lunch while we're out. I'm starving."

CHAPTER 14
EMBER

We stood on the sidewalk in front of Chrys's building, a two-story, brown brick structure with green shutters. Clouds blanketed the sky, the sun's warm rays unable to penetrate the thick layer, and chilly October air whipped through my hair, blowing it into my face. I pulled it back and tugged a band from my wrist with my teeth, but when I tried to tie it into a low ponytail, it slipped through my fingers. It was too short to pull back.

"Dammit." I put the band back on my wrist and tucked my purple locks behind my ears.

Mayhem gave me a quizzical look. "Is there a problem with your hair?"

"An imp gave me a bad haircut." I started toward the steps and paused. "Ash, are there any wards?"

My sister stepped forward and did her thing, sending golden sparkles toward the building. The front walk was clear, but thank the goddess I asked, because Ash's magic clung to the door and windows, revealing a nasty spell.

My lip curled. "I'm beginning to hate earth witches. Can we neutralize it, or do I get to unravel it the fun way...with my sword?"

"What makes you think an earth witch cast this spell?" Mayhem stepped toward the front porch, but Chaos stopped him with a hand on his forearm. "Was Chrys the only magical being residing here?"

"I don't think. I know." I pointed to Ash's magic-revealing sparkles, trailing my finger to the flowerbed beneath a window. "Follow the glitter. The ward is rooted in the ground."

"Fascinating," he said. I didn't detect sarcasm in his voice, but I doubted he found witch magic the slightest bit interesting.

"It's fresh too." Ash examined the hex, her eyes calculating. "Like yesterday fresh. And if my gut is right, it's to keep out witches. The human residents won't feel a thing when they pass through it."

"Her mom did it." My shoulders slumped. "She probably cleared out the apartment already."

"Maybe not." Ash rummaged through her Mary Poppins bag and handed a bowl to Chaos before dumping a few herbs into it. "Grief has a way of paralyzing people. Going through a deceased loved one's belongings is difficult at best. It can also be devastating."

"She put the ward up to keep you away from her possessions until she found the strength to go inside." Chaos held the bowl steady as Ash added three drops of oil, making the potion pop and sizzle.

My sister nodded. "I couldn't bring myself to go inside Cinder's room when we thought she was dead."

"Knowing Discord, she most likely *is* dead." Mayhem started up the steps.

"Whoa. Hold your horses." I grabbed his arm, and prickly tingles shimmied up to my elbow before I let go. "Ash has to deactivate the ward first."

He rubbed his arm where I had touched him, his brow furrowing as if he felt the electric sensation too. "The ward is to keep out witches, which I am not." He opened the door and strode right on in like he owned the place.

"You don't know which apartment is hers," I shouted from the sidewalk.

"Then I will try them all." The door clicked shut behind him.

"Mother effer." I cast my gaze to the left and then the right, making sure no humans were around before I drew my sword. Clutching it in both hands, I raised it above my head, sucking in a breath and steeling myself for the blast of magic I was about to feel.

"Ember, wait." Ash poured a potion on the ground where the spell was rooted. "It'll take a few minutes to dissolve."

"We don't have a few minutes with Mayhem on the loose." I barely heard Chaos say, "I can..." before I brought my blade down, slicing through the hex.

The moment the enchanted silver hit magic, a sharp, vibrating pain shot up my arms and rattled my teeth. The spell popped, creating a flash of blinding light and making my ears ring so loudly I couldn't hear anything else.

Pushing through the pain, I opened the door and strode inside. It took a minute for my eyes to adjust to the dim hallway. I blinked, willing the world back into focus, and when my vision cleared, I found the first door on the left ajar, the jamb busted where the lock had been engaged.

"Are you kidding me? Mayhem!" I whisper shouted.

He strolled into the hall, carrying a bag of candy, his mouth full of chocolate. "That is a human's apartment," he mumbled around the stolen treat.

"That..." I gestured to the busted door. "Is called breaking and entering." I snatched the bag from his hands and shook it. "And this is theft. It's not how we operate."

"Oh my goddess." Ash entered the building, followed by Chaos. "Please tell me no one was home."

"The only lifeform I sensed was a feline, who darted under the sofa the moment I entered." He tried to take the bag from me, so I yanked it away and marched into the apartment.

I set the candy on the counter and returned to the hall, closing the broken door as best I could before glaring at the demon. "You can't just bust into places. There are rules and laws we have to follow, not to mention how dangerous it is to pass through a ward that could have hidden, deadly magic woven through it."

Ash laughed dryly. "Hello, Ms. Pot. Have you met Mr. Kettle?"

She brushed past me, heading to apartment 1E. "We're lucky that ward didn't have an alarm. You both need to chill the eff out and think before you act."

My sister sent her magic-revealing sparkles toward Chrys's door, but they dissipated, a few clinging here and there while the rest dissolved. "There's evidence of an old ward, but it's not active." She pulled out her lock-picking equipment and did her thing.

"A witch of her power wouldn't need one." Mayhem closed his eyes, his lips curving up slightly at the memory before he rested a steely gaze on Ash's back.

Chaos moved to stand behind her, blocking her from Mayhem's view.

"We're in." Ash rose and pushed the door open before stepping inside.

"Is this not breaking and entering?" Mayhem crossed his arms. "Don't you have laws you must obey?" This time I definitely detected sarcasm.

"It's just entering. No breaking involved." I gestured to the door Ash and Chaos had disappeared through. "Go."

He looked down his nose at me. "Ladies first."

I lifted my chin. "Age before beauty, your royal pain in my assness. I'm not letting you out of my sight."

He fought his grin, and I didn't miss the amusement dancing in his eyes before he stepped inside Chrys's apartment. I followed, gently closing the door behind me.

The air hung stagnant, like the doors and windows hadn't been opened for weeks, and dust motes floated in the living room, glinting in the long rays of afternoon sun filtering through the blinds. A book lay open on the coffee table, and Ash peered at the pages, bringing her fingers to her lips on a quick intake of breath.

"Those are the sigils Chrys used to control Shade and Miles." She sank onto the sofa. "Where did she find a grimoire with this kind of power in it?"

I stood next to her and looked at the pages. It felt wrong to have a seat in the living room of our nemesis, so I crouched, leaning my elbows on my thighs. "You're right. We should take this home. It could give us clues about her involvement in this ordeal."

I hovered my hands over the book and recoiled when the sticky funk of dark magic washed over my palms. "It's thick. We need to cleanse it before we handle it."

"Cleanse it of what? It's not dirty." Mayhem slammed the grimoire shut and lifted it up and down as if testing its weight. "It's not thick either. Just a few hundred pages."

I straightened. "Thick with dark magic, smartass."

"If light witches aren't careful, it can seep into our psyches and make us sick." Ash stood and strode toward the kitchen. "But since it doesn't seem to bother you, feel free to carry it home for us."

He dropped it onto the counter. "I'm here for the amulet, not to be your pack mule."

"I'll carry it." Chaos grabbed the book and tucked it under his arm. "Ash, can you locate the artifact?"

Mayhem yanked out a drawer and dumped it on the counter. "We'll find it if we have to tear the place apart."

He pulled on the next drawer, and I popped my hip against it, slamming it shut. "We don't have to tear anything apart. If it's here, Ash will find it. Now, be quiet and let her search."

"'Magical amulet' is so vague. It would help if I knew exactly what I was looking for." She took a deep breath and closed her eyes. "There are so many artifacts in here, it's hard to differentiate them."

"Don't start doubting yourself now." I rubbed her back. "You've got this."

She nodded and stilled, her energy pulling inward as she opened herself to whatever it was she felt when she used this power. Mayhem arched a skeptical brow, his eyes… Honestly, his eyes had been calculating since the moment we brought him into our world.

Without a word, Ash paced across the kitchen toward Chrys's bedroom, and a smile spread across my face. I elbowed Chaos. "Look at her go. I'm so proud of her."

"As am I." He followed her, flipping the light switch on his way into the room.

Mayhem turned to the cabinets, opening each one until he found Chrys's stash of snacks. He stuck his hand into the Twinkie box, ready to steal yet another treat, so I slapped the door hard, bouncing it off his arm.

"Can't you go five minutes without shoving sugar into your mouth?"

In half a nanosecond, his expression morphed from mildly amused to downright scary. His brow slammed down over his eyes, the purple in his irises glowing, his lip pulling into a sneer.

The change in his demeanor barely had time to register in my mind before he moved, his arm jutting out, his thick fingers wrapping around my throat. I gasped, and he squeezed, lifting me from the ground as a sinister growl rumbled in his chest.

His grip tightened, leaving me mere seconds before he crushed my windpipe. The rhythm of my pulse whooshing in my ears quickened, and I prayed to the goddess I could maintain control over my bladder.

"You push me too far, witch." His voice turned gravelly, underworldly. "I am a Prince of Hell, and you will…"

Before he could finish his tirade, I lifted my knee, snatched a dagger from my thigh holster, and shoved the blade two inches into his chest. His eyes widened in shock, and his grip loosened enough for me to drag in a breath as he lowered me to the ground.

"I could snap your neck," he growled.

"Not before I could pierce your heart." I pushed it in a smidge farther.

His eyes locked with mine, and the purple glow faded to a gentle pulse. We stood there, frozen in a draw for what felt like an eternity. His gaze dipped down to my mouth, his eyes tightening as they met mine. I couldn't tell if he wanted to kill me, eat me, or bang my brains out right there in the kitchen. Maybe it was all three.

"Hey, Em?" Ash called. "I found something."

I pulled my blade out an inch. "Truce?"

He loosened his grip, resting his hand at the base of my throat. "For now."

I stepped backward, out of his grasp, and ran the tip of my dagger under the faucet to rinse off his poisonous blood. "Sorry about your shirt."

He glided his finger over the slit I'd made with my blade and shrugged.

"Ember?" Ash called again.

"Coming." I gestured for him to go first, and he conceded, striding into the bedroom like our little standoff hadn't just happened.

I took a step, and my knees nearly buckled. I caught myself on the counter and inhaled a deep, hopefully calming breath while my stomach roiled. There had been nothing little about that standoff at all. He'd gone from being a thorn in my side to giving me a near-death experience in a blink.

Maybe I had pushed him too far.

After two more breaths, I tested my legs. Thankfully, they held, and I put one foot in front of the other, willing my hands to stop trembling as I joined the others in the bedroom.

Or rather...the bathroom.

Chaos and Ash stood on either side of the toilet,

peering into the tank. Mayhem loomed toward it, but Chaos put a hand on his chest.

"That's not…" He leaned forward, and Chaos pushed him back, freeing enough space for me to slide in.

An unassuming red stone rested at the bottom of the tank. Twisted wire created a cage around it, with a long black cord laced through to make it wearable. "Is that it?"

"It's a piece of it," Ash said.

I dunked my hand into the tank to scoop it up, but Ash grabbed my arm. "Don't touch it. Look what it did to Chrys. It drove her mad."

"That's only one theory." I tugged from her grasp. "How else are we going to get it home if we don't touch it? Bring the whole toilet with us?"

"I will carry the amulet," Mayhem said.

"No." Chaos widened his stance, blocking his path to the commode.

"What's the matter, brother? Afraid to be the least powerful prince?"

Chaos let out an irritated sigh. "It's a broken shard, and we don't know which aspects of the magic reside in this piece. Until it's complete, no one touches it."

"We need to contain it." Ash slipped her bag off her shoulder, laying it on the counter before removing the lid from a clear plastic container and dumping out a wad of cotton balls. "We can scoop it up with this and put a ward on it to keep the magic from seeping out."

"How are you going to keep the toilet juice from spilling? It doesn't look watertight. Hold on." I slipped past the demons and returned to the kitchen, rummaging through the drawers until I found what I was looking for.

I returned to the bathroom and clicked a set of tongs triumphantly. Because everyone knew before you used tongs, you had to click them. I didn't make the rules.

"Ready?" I clicked them again.

Ash held up the container. "Do it fast before the magic travels up the tongs."

I grabbed the offending artifact and dropped it into the box. Ash set it on the counter, resting the lid on top before taking out her mixing bowl and three jars of herbs.

"Crappity crap. I'm out of garlic." She held up an empty jar.

"I'm sure there's some in the kitchen. Do you have enough marjoram and patchouli?"

"Plenty." She dumped them into the bowl and crushed them with the back of a spoon.

I paced to the kitchen yet again and located a bottle of garlic powder. When I returned, I found the guys in Chrys's bedroom, going through her drawers. "What are you doing?"

Chaos opened a jewelry box. "Looking for clues."

Mayhem scoffed. "My brother's little witch ordered us out of the room, and he obeys her like a hellhound on a leash."

He slammed the box shut. "She asked us to look for clues."

"Why do I have to keep reminding people we're on the same team?" I strode past them and joined Ash in the bathroom.

She mixed the spell and used a makeup brush to apply the powder to the box before holding her hand toward me. "Cast it together?"

"Of course." I took her hand and focused on the container. "Vessel tight, vim bright, hold the magic until the end of our plight," we said in unison. "As we will it, so mote it be." We sent our energy into the spell, and the powder glowed dark green before flashing once and dissipating.

Ash tapped the plastic, yanking her finger away the moment it made contact. "I think it's good." She tentatively tapped it three more times before picking it up. "It's contained."

Chaos appeared in the doorway with the dark grimoire tucked under his arm. "Would you like me to carry that too?"

Mayhem stood behind him, that same calculating look in his eyes, so I took the container from her. "I'll hold on to this one." No way was he getting his hands on it.

"Will it be enough to convince Discord to cross over?" Ash asked.

"Absolutely not," Mayhem said. "It was his most cherished possession."

I eyed the stone shard. "Fabulous. How do we find the rest of it?"

CHAPTER 15
MAYHEM

Our initial search for the remaining piece of the amulet proved fruitless. After Ember and Ash had neutralized the dark magic coating the stolen grimoire, they had scoured the pages in search of a clue as to where it might be. They'd found nothing, and though they possessed the ability to scry for it, Ember had insisted they slumber before trying. It seemed witches became less powerful the more magic they used, and the sisters, no matter their lineage, were no exception.

My body, in this mortal realm, also required rest, so I had lain in their sister's room. When I awoke three hours later, I went to the living room to watch the television.

Now, I stood outside Ember's doorway, watching her sleep. Silver light from the moon swept across her face like silk, her expression one of serenity. It was an expression I doubted her features could hold if she were awake.

She carried the weight of an entire coven on her shoulders. The tension in her jaw and the tightness of her eyes were the result of being thrust into a position of authority she did not want. And she had assumed the role of High Priestess because of a series of events that began to unfold when the vile Isabel summoned us...used us...with no intention of ever upholding her side of the bargain.

My lip curled at the thought. Isabel had used her wiles to trick us, offering her body to us whenever and wherever we chose. The strength of her magic when I'd lain with her had been intoxicating, but I knew now that it was a ruse. She'd sworn I felt it because we were meant to be. That fate had brought us together, and that she belonged to the three of us. That she would happily sacrifice her soul and that of her first-born if it meant spending eternity with my brothers and me.

How could we have been so stupid?

Looking back now, I could see the warning signs. The lack of good signs. Though my anger with these witches for not allowing me to burn through their adversary and claim her magic still simmered in my soul, I had noticed the way Ash looked at my brother. The admiration in her eyes and the trust in him she exuded were unlike any I had ever witnessed. Not from anyone...especially Isabel.

The same was true about the way Chaos looked at Ash, how he interacted with her. His enamor with her ran deeper than the physical, but to say fate brought us here to be with these witches, that all of this had been set up four hundred years ago...

The idea was not only preposterous, it could be detrimental to my exacting of revenge.

A snort drew my attention back to Ember's bed. She stirred, wiping the drool from her cheek with the back of her hand and rolling to her side to face me, still fast asleep.

She had nearly vanquished me today. To be fair, I had nearly broken her neck, but the fact I'd let my guard down enough to allow her the opportunity was more than alarming. Still...when her knife had entered my chest, mere inches of muscle separating my heart from the would-be blade of my demise, I hadn't felt fear, panic, or even the anticipation of returning home.

No, what I had felt was even more alarming than the fact she could have done it. Admiration and respect had tightened my chest along with the other sensations warming my groin and making my dick harden. She was a formidable opponent, and if her performance in the bedroom was half as skilled as the way she fought, she could be an extraordinary partner.

It was a shame I had to kill her.

I would wait, however. They had enticed me to stay with the promises of fighting fae and making Isabel's descendants pay for her crimes, but the real prize existed in pieces in this realm and these witches had the power to find them all.

The magic of Discord's amulet would be mine, even if I had to absorb it broken shard by broken shard. And my first dose of power lay on the nightstand next to Ember's bed.

Her wards blocked entry to anyone with ill intent. I possessed none toward her at this moment in time, so I crossed the threshold without hesitation.

The second I stepped into her room, a blast of vibration shot into the space. She moved so quickly, had I not been a demon, I would have missed her attack. Reaching under her pillow, she retrieved a nine-inch dagger, which she hurled toward me while simultaneously shooting to her feet. I dodged the blade, and the point stuck in the doorjamb where I had stood.

She exhaled a curse and grabbed a knife from something attached to her bedside table, pointing the blade at me. "Take a step closer, and you can go to Hell."

I raised my hands in a show of innocence. "I mean you no harm."

"No?" She crept around the bed, putting it between us. "Then why are you in my room? And don't you dare say you wanted a little naughty time because I am not interested."

I had to laugh. "As much as I would enjoy ravishing you and making you beg for more, that is not why I'm here."

Her sword hung on the wall above her bed, and she laid the knife on the mattress to retrieve her favorite weapon. "You're the one who'd be begging, mister cocky with a capital C. I'd make you scream my name."

"Don't make promises you can't keep. Nothing gives a demon more pleasure than torturing those who don't hold up their end of a bargain." Though I would love to watch her try, especially with her current state of undress.

Her hair, disheveled from sleep, hung in tangled waves around her face, framing her delicate features. The tightness around her dark brown eyes had returned, and she licked her lips, drawing my attention to her mouth.

My gaze dipped lower, admiring the outline of her nipples through her thin t-shirt, and then sliding down her form to the simple black panties covering the spot I had the sudden urge to lick.

Snapping out of my stupor, I gestured to the enchanted box on her nightstand. "I'm here for the amulet."

"You can't have it." She leaped onto the mattress and grabbed the container before dropping to the floor in front of me. "We're giving it to Discord, so he'll bring our sister and parents back."

I pulled the dagger from the wall behind me and tossed it pommel over tip, catching the handle on its descent. "You feel a sense of loyalty to your family."

"Of course I do." She eyed the blade, clutching her sword in both hands. "Don't you?"

"Not the way you do." I turned the dagger handle toward her and set it on the nightstand before raising my hands once more and backing toward the wall. "Your sister can find things with her mind. What is your special power?"

She took the blade and returned it to the bed, beneath her pillow. "Aside from controlling fire, which we all can do, I don't have one. That's why I learned to fight."

"Are you not envious of Ash? Would you not give anything to possess more magic?"

She relaxed her posture, lowering her arm so the sword pointed at the ground. "I could never be jealous of her. That power belongs to her. She inherited it from our father, and it suits her just like the feeling of a weapon in my hands suits me."

I nodded, regarding her. "Perhaps your ability in battle is your magical gift."

She laughed. "Doubtful."

"Are you sure?"

She opened her mouth to respond, but the words

escaped her. She shook her head, her posture relaxing more. "Aside from my fire, I have to work at everything I do, and apparently, spellcasting needs to be at the top of my list." She waved a hand at the door. "I can't even set up a ward to keep out ill intent."

"I had no ill intent toward you. I simply came to claim what should be mine." I took a step toward her. When she didn't stiffen, I took another. "I passed through your ward with no issue, yet your alarm still activated. Why?"

"The alarm was for anything demonic. I'm going to put this down. Don't make me pick it up again."

"I have no intention to." Though I couldn't shake the temptation of taking the amulet shard she still clutched in one hand.

"Good." She returned her sword to the rack above her bed and stepped toward her dresser, where she put the box into a drawer before taking out a pair of sweats and pulling them on. "Why do you think the amulet should be yours? Discord made the bet and won."

My jaw tightened at the reminder. "Why should he hold more power than me? Than Chaos? We should be the same, equals."

She tilted her head, studying me. "Equal doesn't always mean same."

"How could it not?" I held her mesmerizing gaze. The common dark brown of her irises should have been unremarkable, but as I looked into them, I felt a pull in the core of my being. An invisible tether attempting to form, threatening to drown me in her eyes.

"My sisters and I are equals, but we're very different from each other." She sank onto the edge of the mattress, folding one leg beneath her. "We all have our own strengths and weaknesses, but when we come together, there's no stopping us."

"Does one of you not possess more abilities than the others? Surely your differences, your weaknesses, aren't equal in their detriment." I leaned against the wall, crossing my arms.

Ember sighed, casting her gaze to the ceiling and tilting her head side to side as she thought. "If I had to pick one, now it would be Ash. Our mother had bound her fire magic to try and keep the curse from coming to fruition. Now that the ties have been broken, she's the most powerful witch I've ever met."

"And it doesn't bother you, being magically weaker than your sister?" I couldn't fathom how it could not.

She shrugged. "Not really. She lacks self-confidence, and she's careful to a fault, but she also keeps the coven running and provides protection to my team. We couldn't keep the beasties at bay without her."

"I see."

She arched a brow. "Do you?"

"No."

"I guess that's the difference between light witches and demons. We love our families, and we're loyal to our covens." She picked up her phone and swiped the screen, letting out a relieved sigh before setting it on her nightstand.

"Discord bet against me and won a token that gives unnatural power to its bearer. Chaos allied himself with witches and allowed you to vanquish me back to my prison, denying me of the magic I should have received through my summoning. Whatever love or loyalty I could have felt for my brothers died with their betrayal. They don't want my power to grow."

"Maybe because they're afraid of what you might do with it. Or maybe it's not even about you." She stretched her arms over her head, her cropped shirt lifting above her abdomen, revealing the delicate skin beneath her breasts.

Heat pooled in my groin, and I looked away, contemplating her words. "Do you fear Ash since she came into her power?"

"Not Ash herself." She rose and strode to the dresser again, taking out her standard black clothes and laying them on the surface. "But I do fear the curse and what it could make her do."

"Are you willing to stop her, should we not locate the rest of the amulet in time?"

Her head snapped toward me, her eyes narrowing in warning. "We're going to find it, and you are going to end her curse. Now, it's almost dawn. I'm going to take a shower, and then we'll discuss our next steps. Close the door on your way out and get ready to move."

"Are you not taking a weapon into the bathroom? What if I decide to take you up on your offer to make me scream your name?"

She smiled slyly. "I have more weapons hidden in this house than you can begin to imagine, and next time, I won't hesitate to go all the way to your heart."

My stomach tightened, my heart pounding out a rhythm that said she already had.

CHAPTER 16
EMBER

"That was weird, wasn't it?" I stood in the bathroom towel-drying my hair and talking to my reflection like a crazy person. After the heart-to-heart I'd just had with a *demon prince* and the way I'd warmed to him, I might be certifiable.

Since the moment we'd brought Mayhem into this realm, he and I had communicated by taking jabs and mocking each other. Hell, we'd almost killed each other less than twenty-four hours ago. This was the first real conversation we'd had, and dammit if he didn't show a bit of humanity during it.

I hung the towel on a rack and pulled on my underwear, pausing before I grabbed my pants. I hadn't missed his reaction to seeing me braless and in my skivvies, and dammit again if I hadn't found a smidge of pleasure in his heated gaze.

After shoving my legs into my pants, I grabbed my shirt, pulling it on as I walked back to the bathroom. "Damn sexy demon, and his damn insecurities."

He felt inferior to his brothers. That much was obvious, but I didn't get why. Ash's struggle with self-esteem made sense. Her fire magic had been bound her entire life, and though we'd all tried to make sure she didn't feel less-than, she always did.

As far as I'd seen with Mayhem, he was just as strong as Chaos, though maybe a little rougher around the edges. His mind magic was nothing less than deadly, so if demons really were as evil and human-hating as we thought, it seemed to me that Mayhem was *more* powerful in the brain games department.

I turned on the blow dryer and blasted my hair, running a brush through it as I went. Humanity. Inse-curities. Mayhem had shown me a vulnerability I'd have thought he'd keep to himself. I wished he'd kept it to himself, but here I was feeling an inkling of... something...for a demon.

Was it fondness? Nah, I wouldn't go that far. I still wouldn't hesitate to lob off his head and stab him through the heart, and the lobbing might be why I didn't push my blade all the way in yesterday. That *was* why. He'd had me by the throat, and while I could have vanquished him, his skull would've gone with him and he'd be free from prison and the debt he owed me.

Maybe he wasn't the wicked, selfish son-of-a-bitch hellbent on making our lives as hard as possible that I first thought, but he was still a friggin' demon and he couldn't be trusted.

My hair dried in half the time it used to, and after running my fingers through it, I put on my boots and headed to the living room. A few pale rays of early morning sun provided the only illumination in the space. I flipped the light switch on and paced past the couch and into the kitchen.

Shade had stayed the night with Miles at his house, so I only brewed half a pot of coffee. As it percolated, I stared at the *drip, drip, drip* of liquid falling into the pot and contemplated everything that had been put on hold while we tried to end the family curse.

Shade's house had burned to the ground days... maybe weeks ago. I couldn't tell you how much time had passed since Ash found Cinder's journal and possessed herself with Chaos. The days had bled together into one fuzzy, chaotic mess of mayhem and discord.

Their names sure were appropriate.

I grabbed four mugs from the cabinet and set them on the counter when my phone's ringtone blasted from my pocket, making me jump. I'd forgotten to change it back to silent mode when I woke up.

Spellbound Axe lit up the screen, and I closed my eyes, pinching the bridge of my nose before answering the call. "Hey..." Wariness stretched out the word. "I'm sorry I haven't called you back. I've—"

"Six voicemails, Ember. I've left you six voicemails and sent five texts, and you couldn't be bothered to return one of them." To say my boss sounded beyond pissed would be an understatement. "What could you possibly have going on in your life that you couldn't check in and let me know if you ever planned to come back?"

Battling demons. Solving murders. Trying to stop the fae from taking over Salem. My jaw clenched. "Does it matter?"

"No. You're fired." The vibration on my phone told me she'd ended the call.

"That's what I thought." I shoved it into my pocket, poured myself a cup of socially acceptable chemical dependency, and leaned against the counter.

Ash's laughter drifted into the room, followed by the sound of drawers opening and closing. I was halfway done with my coffee by the time the lovebirds joined me, and Ash gave me a quizzical look as she stepped into the kitchen.

"Where's Mayhem?"

"In Cinder's room. He woke me up before dawn, trying to take the amulet shard from me. I sent him to get ready to move."

Ash flicked her gaze to Chaos before widening her eyes at me. "He's not in there. Chaos checked before we came out."

"He—" I slammed down my mug, sloshing coffee onto the counter. "Are you sure?" Without waiting for an answer, I paced across the room and went into the hall.

"Mayhem!" I shouted, not trying to hide the irritation in my voice. I stomped into Cinder's room. The bedsheets lay in a tangle, and a wet towel had been carelessly dropped on the hardwood. "You slimy, effing snake."

My boots thudded in the hall as I marched into my parents' room, checking the bathroom for good measure on my way out. "That demon is dead."

I strapped on my weapons and sheathed my sword in my back scabbard before returning to the front to find Ash and Chaos waiting by the door.

I barreled down the stairs and yanked my phone from my pocket to call for backup. "I'm going to kill him. I'm going to cut off his effing balls and wear them as earrings."

"There's an image I'll never be able to unsee." Ash locked the upstairs door, and she and Chaos followed me through the library and out the back.

I pressed the phone to my ear, and Shade answered on the second ring. "There's a demon on the loose. I'm sharing my location. Find us."

"We'll be out the door in five."

I pressed End and activated location sharing, which we should have kept on for all of us, all the time. I made a mental note to tell everyone later as I stomped through the parking lot and fumed.

Humanity and vulnerability, my ass. Mayhem had known exactly what he was doing, triggering the alarm on my door and the exits in a fake attempt to take the amulet. I'd been tired last night when I set them, and I'd connected them all to the same spell to use less vim. Setting off my room deactivated the others, and he'd played on my emotions to make me lower my guard.

"Where is he?" I stopped abruptly and whirled to face them, making Ash flinch. "I'm sending him back to prison."

She held up her hands. "Let's take a breath and think before we storm through the entire town and make testicular jewelry. Did he get the amulet?"

My hands balled into fists. "Of course not."

"Okay, that's good." She lowered her arms. "Did he mention something he wanted to do? Somewhere he wanted to go?"

"No. No, we just talked. He's jealous of his brothers and wants to gain more power so they can be equal." Or so he said. He probably made it up so I'd feel sorry for him, the bastard.

Chaos closed his eyes, going utterly still for a

second, two, three, four. "He's close. This way." He turned and strode onto the sidewalk.

"Do we need to drive?" I asked as we followed after him.

He stopped, closing his eyes again and taking a deep breath. "Approximately two miles to the north, I sense his energy."

"You can feel him that far away?" Ash asked.

"We are connected, no matter how unruly he may be."

"We're driving. Load up." I put my sword in the floorboard compartment and started the engine while my sister and her demon climbed in.

Trying my best not to peel out of the alley, I hung a left and followed Chaos's directions to a sheep farm north of town. "Can you cloak us, Ash?" I slid out of my seat and opened the hidey hole to retrieve my sword.

She rummaged through her satchel and shook her head. "We're out."

"Oh well." I slammed the door.

"If anyone sees something they shouldn't, I can make them forget." Chaos walked on my right side, and Ash took up my left.

I wanted to tell him *absolutely not*, but at this point, we might need his mind-melting power. "No one but Mayhem gets hurt."

He chuckled. "I will do my best."

We crept past the farmer's house, clinging close to the wall before darting across to the barn. Two men worked inside, cleaning out stalls and refilling water troughs, so we tiptoed around to the side, my heart hammering in my chest as I devised my plan to vanquish a demon prince.

I would take his head, though after our first imp attack, I knew that wouldn't kill him. He'd run his mouth while I held him by his lush, dark hair. But then, I'd silence him with a dagger to his heart, and his corporeal form would disintegrate before getting sucked through the veil.

I know, I know. I said I'd wear his balls as earrings but come on. That's just gross.

"Is he in the barn?" I whispered.

"No. He's this way." Chaos strode toward the pasture like he owned the place, and there was nothing we could do but follow.

We found Mayhem crouching next to a blob of white and red. More splotches of the same shape and color dotted the field, and I shielded my eyes against the sun rising on the horizon.

"What the actual eff?" I marched toward the demon but stopped short when my gaze landed on the ball of fur. No, not fur...wool. Every sheep in the pasture had been gutted.

A spark of anger tinged with disgust lit in my belly, the flames rising to my chest. I grabbed Mayhem's shoulder and shoved, but he could have been a boulder sitting amongst the death and destruction.

"You slaughtered a herd of sheep?" I side-kicked him in the back, and he rose, his hands covered in blood. "You disgusting, lying snake."

"I did not kill these animals," he said.

"Bullshit." I unsheathed my sword. "Ash, freeze him."

Her shoulders crept toward her ears. "Yeah, that spell won't work on him. We'd have to use a containment circle."

"Oh, for Hecate's sake." I reared back, gripping my sword like a baseball bat.

"Mayhem speaks the truth." Chaos wiped his hands on a rag Ash handed him. "Their livers are gone. This was the work of the fae."

"That's okay." I rocked on my feet, tensing for attack. "He still left the house unescorted. It's reason enough for me to vanquish him."

"Hold on." Ash laid a hand on my shoulder. "If you send him back to hell now, we'll never know why he left or what brought him here."

"I don't give a shit." My muscles coiled, the tension in my arms and shoulders ready to swing with all my might.

I moved the sword half an inch when Chaos grabbed my wrist in one hand, yanking the sword from my grasp with the other. The nerve of this guy! If my sister wasn't in love with him, I'd vanquish them both.

I grabbed a dagger and lunged at Mayhem. Chaos caught me around the waist and dragged me back, holding me tightly against his chest. "Ash, get your demon under control."

Her face scrunched. "He's not the one who's out of it."

"Are you kidding me right now?" I struggled against Chaos's hold, but it was no use. I might as well have been trapped beneath a collapsed building. "He broke the rules and left the house. He betrayed our trust."

Mayhem had the audacity to laugh. "You made no such stipulation last night."

"It was implied," I said through clenched teeth, struggling again against the demon's strength.

"Implications aren't rules, and you never trusted me. There was nothing to betray." He lifted one shoulder dismissively.

"You lied to me. You told me stories to make me feel compassion for you so you could get out the door without setting off the alarm."

His brow furrowed. "Demons are known to lie, but everything I said to you was truth." He turned to Ash and held up his bloody hands. "Do you have another rag?"

She took one from her bag and gave it to him.

"Whether or not you had permission to leave aside, what brought you here?"

"I sensed a rift while the rest of you were indisposed, so I came to investigate." He gestured to an invisible spot ten yards away. "It's rather large, and based on the number of dead sheep, I'd say at least five fae soldiers came through. I would seal it if I were you."

Ash tugged two bottles from her bag and cast a magic-location spell to make the rift visible. A horizontal tear in the veil stretched at least six feet wide and three feet tall. "Whoa. That's huge. I'm going to need help with this one."

Chaos released his hold, and I pointed at Mayhem. "Don't move," I said before taking my sister's hand.

She blew the mending powder onto the rift and opened to me, allowing her energy to flow out of her hand and into mine before we recited the spell in unison. The edges of the rift stitched themselves back together, leaving a three-by-two hole in the fabric of reality.

"Again," Ash said as she took another bottle from her bag and blew the powder toward the tear.

A surge of power filled my psyche, making me gasp. Chaos had taken Ash's other hand, sharing his magic with us.

"It feels good, doesn't it?" Mayhem stood next to me and wiggled his brows. "But you're getting filtered magic. Imagine getting it right from the source." He held his hand toward me, and for half a second, I was tempted to take it.

What little he'd shared with me during the summoning had been intoxicating enough, so instead, I shoved my hand into my pocket and focused on the rift. Chaos's and Ash's magic spun in my chest, hers calm and serene, his...well, it was chaotic. There was no other way to describe it.

I let it meld with my power, and we recited the incantation two more times, giving it all we had. The tear slammed shut, the fibers of the veil weaving together, blocking any more giant bugs from getting through.

I tugged from my sister's grip, breaking the connection, and heaved in a breath. "That was a doozy."

My head spun, but I couldn't tell if it was because of the rush of demonic magic dissipating in my system or the effort it had taken to seal the rift.

"What the hell?" a gruff voice said from behind us. The sound of a shotgun cocking followed, and I spun to find the men from the barn glaring at us. The one in brown coveralls lowered the barrel, pointing it directly at me.

"Now might be a good time for some mind magic," I said under my breath as I held up my hands, my fire power building, rolling from my chest to my arms. "Chaos, Ash, do your thing."

The guy in a blue t-shirt turned on his buddy, landing a punch square on his jaw. Coveralls stumbled, losing his grip on the gun and dropping it. He picked it up again and slammed the stock into Blue Shirt's stomach.

"Run," Ash said, grabbing me by the arm, but I rooted myself to the ground, refusing to budge.

If Chaos and Ash had been doing *their* thing together, they would have made Coveralls hand over the gun before Chaos scrambled both their minds, making them forget the last ten minutes.

But no, this wasn't their thing. This was Mayhem's work.

"Turn it off." I reached for my sword, but the demon caught me by the wrist and twisted my arm behind my back with so much force, my bones nearly snapped.

"Focus your violence on the ones causing trouble. I'll help you." Mayhem shoved me toward the men, and Blue Shirt clocked me in the eye.

Pain exploded across my cheek, and I stumbled, pressing my hands to my face to make sure nothing was broken.

"We don't hit women, asshole." Coveralls leveled the gun at Blue Shirt.

Normally, if a man laid a finger on me, I'd be the

one breaking arms. And that gun? I'd have ripped it from his hands and slammed the butt into his temple, sending him to Sleepyville, whether Mayhem had control of his mind or not.

Instead, a sense of calm washed over me. I took two steps back and raised my hands in a show of innocence. "Hey guys, let's talk this out. There's no need for violence."

"The hell there isn't." Coveralls fired, the sound nearly busting my eardrums as Blue Shirt flew backward, landing on the ground with a thud.

"Release them, brother." Chaos grabbed Mayhem by the throat and lifted him...all two-hundred-plus pounds of him...two inches from the ground. "Or I will help Ember vanquish you."

"Nobody needs to get vanquished." I patted Chaos on the shoulder. "I'm sure we can all come to an agreement if we talk it out."

Chaos cut his gaze to me, narrowing his eyes before turning a steely glare on his brother. "Release *her*."

Her? Was another human here that I hadn't seen?

"As you wish, *brother*." He spat out the last word.

My head spun, and I blinked rapidly as Chaos lowered him to the ground.

"Jonah!" Coveralls shouted and tossed the gun aside. He raced to the man he'd shot, dropping to his knees and sobbing. "I'm so sorry. I don't... I don't know what happened. Someone call an ambulance."

"Ash, call Patrice." I squeezed my eyes shut, shaking my head and attempting to clear my mind. What the hell had just happened? I was about to grab my sword and force Mayhem to let them go, but then...

All I'd wanted was for everyone to stop fighting.

Had Ash cast a calming spell on me? She'd done it before when I'd gotten unruly, but it had been ages. Believe it or not, I had my temper under control way more now than I did five years ago.

I scratched the back of my head. "Ash, did you...?"

"Patrice is five minutes away." She opened her satchel, dropping to her knees beside the wounded man, and all I could do was watch in confusion. "Ember, come put pressure on the wound."

"Yeah. Okay." I joined her on the ground, and Coveralls sat back on his heels.

"I couldn't have done that. I would never." He blinked at me, his eyes dazed. I knew the feeling. "Who shot him?"

"You did." I pressed a towel to the top part of the wound while Ash used tweezers to pick the buckshot out of the lower half. "Guns are dangerous."

"So are humans who meddle in magical affairs." Mayhem crossed his arms, and Chaos closed his eyes for a long, irritated blink.

Anger boiled in my gut at the audacity of the

demon. How many times would I have to tell him before he finally got it through his thick skull? "You shouldn't have done that."

He inclined his chin. "He would have killed you otherwise."

"No, he wouldn't have."

He scoffed. "You think you can outrun a shotgun blast?"

Clink, clink, clink. The tiny pieces of metal landed in Ash's bowl.

Footsteps, muffled by the grass, grew closer, and I lifted my gaze to find Shade and Miles *finally* arriving.

"Holy shit. What happened?" Shade asked.

"Mayhem happened." My voice sounded more like a growl. "Can you cloak this area in case any more farmhands decide to check on the sheep?"

"How big...?" He scanned the field, taking in the carnage of the lambs. "Whoa. Mayhem did all that?"

"I did not decimate the livestock." Mayhem straightened his spine, dropping his arms to his sides but keeping his muscles flexed. "I located the rift where the fae are getting through, and I believe some thanks are in order."

"You—" I clamped my mouth shut. There was no use arguing with a sociopath. His twisted perception of reality kept him from thinking like a normal person...and by normal, I meant people without murderous tendencies.

Gray fog rolled around us as Shade did his thing, and I moved the towel to a different part of the wound so Ash could pick out more shrapnel. Coveralls hauled himself off the ground and stumbled toward his discarded shotgun.

"Miles, can you take over?" I motioned for him and lifted my hands so he could apply pressure. Jumping to my feet, I darted around them just as Coveralls picked up his weapon.

"Who shot Jonah?" Bleary-eyed and snotty-nosed, he swung the barrel toward me, but this time my brain actually worked.

I grabbed the gun and wrenched it from his hands before twisting his arm behind his back the same way Mayhem had held me before my thoughts went haywire. "Shade, grab a binding spell so I can neutralize this guy. He's caused enough trouble."

"On it." He dug through Ash's bag and tossed me the bottled spell.

"Standing tall or on your knees, in the name of the goddess, I force your ass to freeze." I dumped the powder onto Coveralls' head. His muscles seized, and a squeak emitted from his throat before he fell face first into the dirt.

I rolled him over so he wouldn't suffocate and dusted off my pants before whirling toward the demons. "Would either of you care to tell me what the hell just happened?"

CHAPTER 17
MAYHEM

The healer approached with another witch and stopped to peer at her phone. "The map shows they're right in front of us, but this is an empty field. Shade, is that your doing?"

The shadow witch took a deep breath and lifted a hand toward the women. His fog rolled outward, grass that once appeared gray turning green as the cloak extended and engulfed the witches.

"Oh... Oh!" Patrice ran toward the injured man and opened her healer bag. "How much blood has he lost?"

Ash and Miles stood, giving her room to perform her duties. "Not much," she said. "Thankfully, the gunman isn't a good shot." She sanitized her hands with another chemical possessing an offensive stench and offered the bottle to Miles, who did the same.

"Whoa. That's..." The other witch stared at the

field of mutilated animals before blinking up at me. "Who are you?"

"My name is—"

"That's just Dave." Ember walked toward me, her tone dismissive. "He's Mark's brother. You met Mark, right? Ash's boyfriend."

"Yes. Hi, I'm Inga." She offered a timid wave.

"Dave?" I furrowed my brow.

"Just go with it," Chaos said under his breath.

Ember cleared her throat. "He prefers David, but whatever. At least we don't call him Dick. That would be more appropriate."

I was about to respond that I in no way resembled a phallic appendage when Inga asked, "Where are you from?"

"The deepest depths of Hell."

A maniacal laugh escaped Ember's throat. "Texas. He means Texas. Have you ever been? It gets so hot, you feel like you're in Hell. Humid too."

Chaos moved closer and said, "She can't know who we are. I'll explain later."

I regarded him before cutting my gaze to Ember. She mouthed the word *please*, and I suppressed a smile. I could go along with their ruse...since she begged.

"I'd say it's a pleasure to meet you, Inga, but under the circumstances..." I gestured to the man and then the field.

"What happened?" Patrice asked.

"Well, see..." Ember's expression revealed she scrambled for an answer, so I assisted her.

"A large rift formed, and several fae got through, slaughtering the sheep in their wake. This gentleman..." I motioned to the frozen gunman. "He accused the victim of disemboweling his flock and decided an eye for an eye was the best course of action. Sadly, we couldn't stop him from firing, but Ash and Ember tended to his wounds while awaiting your arrival."

The sisters blinked at me three times before Ember recovered. "Sad story, isn't it? Will he survive?"

"He'll be fine." She removed a pair of gloves and rose to her feet, eyeing me suspiciously as she picked up her bag. "I left a few marks from the buckshot, so it'll look like he barely grazed the skin."

She cut her gaze to Chaos, then Ash, and back to Ember. "I hope you froze him fast enough that he won't remember."

Ember ushered Inga toward Patrice. "Thanks so much for your help."

"A hospital could have done the same thing. Is there anything else...?" She glanced at Chaos and me.

"I know, and we're sorry to have bothered you." She lowered her voice. "Shade dropped the cloak too soon and got a little spell-happy, freezing them both. We were afraid he'd die before the binding wore off if we waited to call an ambulance."

"I..." He stiffened, his lips forming a thin line, and I held in another laugh. "Do you have any idea the amount of effort it takes to shadow an entire field like this?"

"You're doing a great job." Ember flashed a tight-lipped smile, her message less than subtle, before turning to Patrice. Any news from your end? More murders or beasties getting through?"

"You haven't heard?" She reached into her bag and pulled out a smaller one. "A couple who'd been living beneath an overpass were found hidden in some nearby brush. It happened overnight between Salem and Boston."

"They're organizing," I said. "We must find the ones who did this."

"Here." Patrice offered the smaller bag to Ash. "I bottled some pain powders and healing creams. I need to get back to my workshop to make more. It sounds like we'll need them."

"Thanks, Patrice. Keep me posted." Ember lifted a hand as they walked away, and as they exited the cloaked area, she spun toward me. "I want answers. What makes you say they're organizing? If they're hoping to take over this realm, don't they already have a plan?" She lifted a finger, counting each question. "How do we find invisible preda-tors? Why did they kill these sheep? What the hell were you thinking turning these men on each other, and which one of you messed with my mind?"

I attempted to suppress my smile, but the fire in her eyes and the emotion in her words made a strange flitting sensation rise from my stomach to my chest like a swarm of moths attempting to escape, attracted to the flames of Ember.

She put her hands on her hips. "Is this funny to you?"

"Not in the slightest."

"I can't hold this shadow much longer," Shade said.

Ember paced four steps in one direction before returning to her starting point. "Let's go. I need food before I can think clearly. Chaos..." She jabbed a finger toward me. "Not you. Chaos, can you *gently* make them forget we were ever here?"

"Of course," he said.

"Ash, stay with him and make sure he behaves. We'll meet you at the van." She jerked her head toward the front of the farm. "Demons first."

"Are you sure? I rather enjoy watching you walk away."

She faltered. If only for a fraction of a second, she lost her steely composure, showing that my words affected her as I intended. "Move it."

For some Hades-knew-why reason, I did as she commanded and returned to the van, climbing into the front passenger seat to await the others. Ember paced outside the vehicle, talking to herself in a voice too quiet for me to make out her words.

Apparently, Shade had given her a portable shadow spell because, while he stayed behind with my brother, the world outside our bubble remained grayscale. I didn't see the others approach. One second, we were alone, and the next, Chaos, Ash, Shade, and Miles stood outside the van.

It was no wonder shadow magic was a highly coveted power for demons to possess. Imagine the hysteria we could cause—in this realm and ours—if we could remain undetected. I had met many witches in my eternal existence, but the concentration of power in this small coven made them the greatest I had ever witnessed.

And Ember… It seemed I couldn't get enough of her.

We parked in the lot behind their home and walked three blocks to a restaurant. Shade returned to Miles's home under Ember's order to bottle more shadow magic. He had protested, as he tended to do when he wasn't involved in the coven planning.

I understood the frustration of being left out. I was always the last to learn of Lucifer's plans, *if* I learned of them at all. But Shade held no position of authority in the coven. He was not of the ruling bloodline, so he had no valid argument. I was a Prince of Hell. I belonged to the royal bloodline. Lucifer and my brothers had no acceptable reason for leaving *me* out, yet they did it all the time.

I refused to dwell on it. Once I obtained the amulet, I would show them power. Let them cast me out if they chose. I could build my own army, be king of my own realm.

And I could take Ember as my queen.

We stepped inside the restaurant, and a plethora of savory aromas tickled my senses, making my stomach growl. A young woman with blonde hair and jewelry in her nose greeted us at the door. Her nametag read Stacey.

"Welcome to the Twisted Thistle. Table for four?" she asked. "How about this one by the window?"

Ember shook her head. "That one in the back corner, please."

Stacey giggled. "You must be locals then. I've only lived here a couple of months. Come on." She picked up four menus and led the way to the table Ember had requested.

Long and rectangular, it had cushioned benches on either side rather than chairs. Ash slid across one, and Chaos sat next to her. I waited for Ember to do the same, but she cocked her head at me instead.

"I'd rather not be pinned in." I gestured for her to sit.

"Neither would I." She crossed her arms, so I did the same.

"Would you prefer a table?" Stacey asked. "There's an open one in the middle over there."

"Sit, brother," Chaos said. "I tire of your stubbornness."

"And I tire of your arrogance." I glared at him before lowering onto the bench and making room for Ember.

She sat next to me, and as she adjusted her position, her thigh rested against mine. The moths, having gone dormant on the way here, flitted back to life in my chest. What a strange effect this witch had on me.

"Can you move over? Half my ass is hanging off the seat." Ember wiggled, her left hip rubbing against mine.

My stomach tightened, and though I enjoyed the sensation, I moved away, breaking the physical contact between us lest I lift her over my shoulder and carry her to the Underworld.

How I had gone from despising all witches to desiring this one in a matter of days, I had no clue. She was nothing like any woman I had ever met, and perhaps that reason alone had enamored me. She certainly didn't use her wiles to try and seduce me, yet a seductress she was, nevertheless.

Maybe it was her element that called to me. She commanded fire as if she were born in Hell, her power more potent than any mortal's I could recall...aside from her sister. Ash could be the strongest of them all, yet Ember expressed no envy.

She must have kept it buried deep in her soul.

Once the amulet belonged to me, I could make her more powerful than every witch in her coven combined. Together, we could rule this world and the Underworld.

"Hello?" Ember's voice and her two snaps directly in front of my face drew me from my thoughts. "Earth to Dave. What do you want to drink?"

"The blood of my enemies." I cast my gaze to Stacey, who stood at the table holding a pen and a notepad.

She giggled. "You're a funny one. I always wanted a man who could make me laugh."

"You can have him," Ember said. "And he'll have iced tea like the rest of us."

"You got it." She wrote on her pad before smiling at us. "Y'all make a cute couple."

Ember laughed dryly. "We most definitely are *not* a couple."

"Oh, I'm sorry." Her smile faded, but I couldn't suppress mine.

A cute couple... Cute wasn't the word I would have used, but Stacey's words stirred the moths in my soul.

She turned but hesitated, swiveling back toward

us. "Is there anything I need to do to prepare for Halloween? I hear this town gets crazy packed."

Ash's eyes grew wary. "Take a vacation if you can. Seriously."

"I would if I could. Tuition is ridiculous since I'm not from Massachusetts, but I really wanted to attend Salem State." She shrugged. "So here I am."

"Where are you from?" Ash asked.

Tracey smiled proudly. "Houston, Texas. Born and raised."

"Ah. Hell on Earth," I said.

She looked at me with questions in her eyes. "It's not so bad if you don't mind the humidity... Oh, I get it!" she laughed. "Yeah, it can be hotter than Hell in the summertime. I'll be right back with your drinks." She disappeared through a swinging door.

"Why do you call me Dave?" I perused the restaurant's offerings, not bothering to lift my gaze. I could feel her irritation with me rolling off her skin in waves, and I hadn't yet decided if I should make it worse or relent to her yet again.

"I suggest you don't speak until I have some food in me. Hangry Ember doesn't know how to be nice." She turned her menu over and scanned the backside.

"I didn't realize you ever tried to be." It appeared I'd decided to make it worse. I simply couldn't help myself when it came to her.

She cast a sideways glance at me, her mouth tightening as if she were trying, in this moment, to be nice.

"As far as anyone else needs to know, you and I are fire witches," Chaos said. "I'm from Maine, and apparently you're now from Texas."

"You're lying to your coven?" I turned to Ember, and her nostrils twitched as she silently stewed.

"Just a few lies here and there." Ash glanced at her sister. "We're mostly omitting the important details, which I know..." She held up her hands. "Lying by omission is still lying, but here we are."

Stacey returned with four large glasses of iced tea and took our food orders. Ember asked for a hamburger containing beef and a fried egg. Based on my limited experience with modern food, the combination sounded odd, yet interesting.

"I'll have the same." I handed the menu to Stacey, and Ember side-eyed me, her nostrils flaring again. How my request for the same meal as hers could be upsetting, I couldn't fathom. Perhaps I should back off and let her cool down before resuming our normal banter.

We sat in silence until our food arrived. Ember used a serrated knife to cut her burger in half before taking a bite. While it was massive in size compared to her hands, mine were nearly twice as big as hers. I picked up the whole sandwich and took a bite.

The moment my teeth sank into it, the egg yolk

burst and half the contents fell out the back of the bun in a heap. Mayonnaise coated my fingers, and gooey cheese dangled from my chin.

Ember snorted. "Did you think I cut it in half to eat like a dainty lady? Now you'll have to finish it with a fork and knife."

I chewed the surprisingly tasty combination and swallowed before scooping the mess from my plate with my fingers and shoving it into my mouth.

She shrugged. "Or do it the heathen way. It suits you."

I wiped my hands and face with a napkin and sipped my tea, giving her ample time to get food into her stomach. When she finished half the burger, I set down my glass. "My reason to believe the fae are organizing is this..."

"Stop." She wagged a finger at me. "What you did out there, making those men violent... That's not allowed. We protect the humans. We don't hurt them."

"Those men were already violent in nature. I barely sent a suggestion to them before they turned on one another." I used a fork to scoop a bite of egg and beef.

"It doesn't matter." She gestured between herself and Ash. "We're light witches. You have to at least pretend to care about human life if we're going to get through this."

"But I don't care about it."

She threw her hands in the air and dropped them on the table. "Are you sure we can't break the curse without him?"

"Positive," my brother answered. "I'd have done it already if there were any other way."

"Fine. Just..." She rubbed her temples. "Don't do it again, okay? I'm sure you want to get rid of me as much as I want you gone, so work with us. Please."

That word again. Every time she directed it toward me, it felt like silk running over my skin. "I will try. I swear."

Her shoulders slumped. "Sadly, I know that's the best I'll get from a demon."

Indeed it was. "I believe the fae are organizing because the latest two bodies were hidden. They targeted those who would not be missed, fed out of sight, and removed their leftovers from plain view."

She curled her lip. "They're humans, not leftovers. Try to show a shred of decency."

"I'm the most indecent man you'll ever meet."

Her pheromones flared at my words, the intoxicating scents of campfire and sandalwood making my mouth water. She cleared her throat. "No kidding."

"Their methods are evolving, but I don't believe organizing is the right word." Chaos laid his fork and knife on his empty plate. "If it were the greater fae horde behind the attack, they'd have struck in full force by now."

"I see your point." I drummed my fingers on the table. "It must be a smaller faction. Someone who has fallen out of favor with the king. Doesn't Argon have a half-brother?"

Chaos nodded. "Ignacus. He was never afforded the training of a true fae prince, and this invasion reeks of inexperience, especially his choice of Salem. The veil may be thinnest here, but the coven is the strongest."

"Indeed it does. And he is unaware that two of the three Princes of Hell currently reside in the town he has chosen to invade." I couldn't fault Ignacus for trying. Though born of royal blood, his mother was a mere servant, so the king had never taken him seriously. Invading another land to claim it as his own was a logical move.

"How do you know so much about the fae?" Ember asked.

"The same way you learned about demons," Chaos said. "With research and experience."

Ash rubbed her forehead. "So there's not going to be a full-scale invasion?"

"It depends on how many followers he was able to amass." I laid my napkin across my plate, putting my exploding lunch to rest.

Ember shoved her plate away. "Are we talking twenty? Two hundred? Two thousand?"

"Could be," I said.

"Which?"

"Any or all."

"Hey, y'all." Stacey stood before our table, clasping her hands. "I'll get these plates out of your way, and I was wondering if you'd mind closing out. My shift is over, and I've got to get to class."

"Yeah. Of course." Ember handed her a card, and she tugged a machine from her belt, tapping the plastic rectangle against it before handing both to Ember.

"Thanks for coming in."

"Thank you." Ember handed the machine to Stacey and slid off the bench. "Let's continue this chat at home. I have even more questions now."

CHAPTER 18
EMBER

Way too many tourists milled about the streets for us to continue our conversation outside, so we walked most of the way home in silence. Ash slowed down as we passed an antique shop, but I kept going full speed ahead. One of her jobs in the coven was perusing the local shops and confiscating any artifacts that contained real magic.

"Ember," she shouted, but I kept walking.

"We don't have time for that now," I said over my shoulder before returning my gaze to the pair of demons in front of me.

"Ember!" she nearly screeched, stopping me mid-stride.

I whirled toward her as she jutted her thumb toward the window and mouthed *there's a gnome.*

"Oh for Hecate's sake." I started to call for the guys, but what good would they do? Gnomes were a breed all their own, not demonic, not fae or vampire either. They were just venomous little pests who lived amongst the elves across the veil, tending to their gardens, but digging up ours every chance they got.

Ash disappeared into the shop, and I followed right behind. The dim lighting inside starkly contrasted the bright afternoon. I blinked, trying to force my eyes to adjust, when a two-foot-tall ball of fur and blubber darted past me and headed down the book aisle.

Ash linked arms with Betty, the shop owner with soft pink hair and more laugh lines than I could count, and led her toward the back corner, far away from me and the annoying little bugger chewing on the corner of a children's book.

He spat out the paper, wiping his tongue with his grubby hands in disgust, and I reached beneath my jacket for my knife. Gripping the handle, I scanned the ceiling and corners, making sure Betty hadn't invested in security cameras since the last time I was here. She hadn't, so I crept toward the gnome, doing my best not to startle him.

The door opened, making a bell chime, and Chaos called, "Ash?"

At the sound of his deep voice, the gnome jumped, startled. His gaze locked on me, and he growled, peeling his lips back to show me his cat-like teeth. He scurried toward me, completely unafraid of the knife-wielding witch who towered over him.

I grabbed him by the scruff of his neck, but the bugger wiggled and kicked and grabbed hold of my sleeve, giving himself enough leverage to rip from my grasp. He hit the ground with a thud, but before I could get another handful of fur, he sank his teeth into my leg, the sharp points penetrating my pants and breaking the skin.

"Goddess dammit!" Searing pain surged through my calf, the venom working its way toward my veins. I brought the knife down into his back, and he yelped, releasing my leg. Yanking the blade out, I pressed my boot onto his torso and shoved the knife into his heart.

"Oh my! Is everything okay out there?" Betty hurried as fast as her arthritis would allow, and I yanked off my jacket, wrapped it around the bloody carcass, and picked it up.

"Oh." She stopped, pressing a hand to her chest. "Ember? What...?"

I looked at Ash and the guys and then at the bundle in my arms. "A rat. Huge. It was gnawing on a book."

"Your leg. You're bleeding." She pointed to my blood-soaked pants.

"It bit me, but I'll be fine. I'll just take this out the

back and toss it in the dumpster for you." I limped around her.

"Let me get you a bandage." She patted me on the shoulder.

"I'll take care of her, Betty." Ash wrapped an arm around my shoulders. "You might want to mop up the mess before a customer slips in it."

"You're right dear. Come back when you can. I set aside some things for you." She held the door to the storage room open for us. "Make sure the lock clicks on your way out."

"Will do."

"There's a small rift in the corner." Chaos pointed to our right.

"Ash, can you handle it while I get rid of *this*?" I sneered at the bloody bundle in my arms.

"Sure thing."

I took six steps out the door and dropped the wad of gnome...kicking it for good measure. Fire ignited in the core of my being, and I let it build, allowing it to roll down my arm and gather in my palm until I held a massive fireball.

"I sure hope no one is watching," Ash muttered, pulling the door shut as she stepped outside.

Frankly, with gnome venom climbing up my leg and my favorite jacket about to burn to bits, I really didn't care. I tossed the sphere of flames onto my jacket and gave the bitty beastie a one-fingered salute. "That's for ruining my clothes, you little shit."

The gnome and my jacket turned to ashes in seconds, and I hobbled away, the feeling of icepicks jabbing into my leg making me cringe with each step.

"I can carry you if—" Chaos began.

"Don't touch me." I glanced at Mayhem, expecting a taunting remark, but his blank expression looked scarier than I'd ever seen him.

Okay, maybe scary wasn't the right word because I wasn't afraid of him in the slightest. Even when he'd had me by the throat, he'd squeezed *just* hard enough to make breathing difficult...not impossible. He'd been angry, sure, but he wouldn't have killed me. Something about his energy...the way he looked at me...said it was true.

Or maybe the gnome venom was affecting my brain.

The icepicks in my leg jabbed harder and harder, moving up to my knee and burrowing into the joint. A simple cringe was no longer enough to express my pain. My face contorted, my suppressed groan coming out as a wheeze.

"Do you..." Chaos started again.

"Let her walk." Ash caught up to me and whispered, "Seriously though, do you need help?"

I couldn't bend my knee, my calf swelled until it felt like it would bust out of my pants, and the icepicks now felt like they were hooked to a generator. "I'm fine. Keep an eye on the wild one so he doesn't try to escape while I'm not able to outrun him."

She fell back to join the demons, and I forced myself to hobble the last three yards to our building. The back steps posed a challenge since I couldn't bend my knee. Luckily there were only three and my hip still worked. I leaned to one side and swung my stiff leg up to the next stair, hauling myself up with a tight grip on the handrail.

I limped inside, down the hall, and into the library to peer at the stairs. No way could I make it up to our apartment, so I hopped on one leg to Ash's desk and gingerly rested my butt on the surface. "I'll wait down here while you mix the antivenom."

"Nonsense. You won't be comfortable." Without warning, Mayhem scooped me into a cradle carry, my stiff right leg sticking up as if I were posing for a social media *look how great my life is* post.

I'd like to say shock and pain kept me from protesting, and they did play a role in my temporary submission. But the effortless way he lifted me and held me close to his chest gave me the warm fuzzies in more places than one.

I held onto his neck, bracing myself for the pain when my leg knocked against the wall on our ascent. But he angled me just right, taking the steps sideways and making it all the way to the living room without jostling me in the slightest.

He laid me on the couch, sinking to his knees next to me, his stoic expression still unreadable. Was he angry at me? At the gnome? Or was he indifferent? Perturbed? Who knew?

Brushing my hair off my face, he leaned toward me, and for half a second, I thought he might kiss my forehead. "I will eradicate the entire species for what that one did to you."

Angry at the gnome. Got it. "There's no need to commit genocide. Ash will have me good as new in a few minutes."

"You should have called for me. I would never have let it hurt you." The intensity in his eyes said he meant it. *Yikes.*

I laughed and winced, the movement ramping up the electricity in the icepicks. "First of all, I didn't need help. I've battled way bigger beasties than that. And second—yes, there is a second this time—you had no problem letting the fae soldier knock me around...and you nearly snapped my neck...so I'm not buying what you're selling."

"Hmpf." He rose and tugged my boot off before grabbing the hem of my pants and ripping them open from my ankle to the top of my thigh.

"I guess I won't be salvaging those." I leaned my head back and closed my eyes. With the pressure on my leg gone, the icepicks relented a little, but the swollen, dark purple sausage it had become made my stomach turn.

"You want to keep them as a reminder of the time you were bested by a two-foot ball of fur?"

I lifted one lid to see his teasing smile. There was the Mayhem I knew.

"Here we go." Ash padded into the room, carrying a glass of bright yellow liquid. Chaos followed, a copper bowl in one hand, a rag in the other.

She handed me the glass. "Drink up. This one requires two parts."

I did as instructed and drank the potion. It tasted like lemongrass and relief, cooling my insides and taming the electrical current running through my leg. Chaos set the bowl on the coffee table, and Ash dipped in the rag before rubbing the concoction, which had the consistency of pudding, over the bite and up my leg.

As the magic did its thing, drawing out the venom and easing the pain, I let out a long sigh. Mayhem watched intently from a chair, and Chaos cleaned— yes, cleaned—the mess Ash had made in the kitchen.

"From now on, I'm not leaving the house without sigils. Thicker skin, resistance to venom. Those are easy ones, right?"

Ash dropped the rag into the bowl and rose. "I can do them with my eyes closed."

"That's our next step then." I pushed to sitting, the swelling already subsiding. "Sigils for me, you, Shade, and Miles. We'll only activate them when we need them."

"I can do that." She carried the bowl to the kitchen and washed the dishes before bringing me a beer. "You look like you could use it."

I laughed and accepted the bottle. "We all could."

My leg returned to its normal size and color, and I rotated my ankle, bending my knee to work out the rest of the stiffness before sitting up fully and resting my feet on the floor. "Okay, guys. What else do you know about Ignacus the Ignorant?"

CHAPTER 19
EMBER

"He sees his chance to build a kingdom, and he's taking it." Mayhem shrugged as if invading our realm and slaughtering us all was a completely normal thing to do. "It's not uncommon for those with power to prey on the weaker species."

"Weaker?" I shot to my feet and wobbled on my bare leg. My skin had absorbed all the magical pudding Ash had smeared on it, but it seemed my muscles hadn't fully recovered. I fell backward onto the couch, straightening my spine the moment my butt made contact with the cushion and scooting forward to the edge. "We are not weaker than a bunch of overgrown bugs."

He arched a brow. "Their exoskeletons are nearly impenetrable, their soldiers are invisible, and their saliva is venomous." He leaned toward me, resting his elbows on his knees. "You thought the gnome venom was bad? If a fae bites you, you'll be dead in minutes."

I scooted down the couch, closer to my verbal sparring partner. "Been there, done that, and I'm still around to show off the t-shirt. They're hard to kill, not impossible."

"Hard for you and Ash. For the others?" He gestured toward the door. "A millimeter shy of impossible."

"Don't underestimate the witches of Salem," Chaos said. "When they work as a team, they are a force to be reckoned with."

"And we won't allow the bugs to wipe out human-ity." I straightened my spine. "This is *our* realm."

"They won't wipe you out." Mayhem leaned back, steepling his fingers. "The fae lack an enzyme required to exist in this realm...one that your livers produce. They'll keep you as livestock, breeding you, slaugh-tering you, taking only your livers, and disposing of you like garbage."

"There's a lovely thought." I crossed my legs and massaged the injured one to spread the antidote through my muscles. I needed to move. My brain worked better when I walked. "And let me guess. The sheep don't produce enough of the enzyme to sustain them. That's why they slaughtered the entire herd."

"Precisely."

"We need to find the rest of the amulet." Ash sat on the arm of Chaos's chair. "With any luck, we can summon Discord and mend the veil before Ignacus and his followers pass through."

"Yes." Mayhem moved forward again, his knee resting against mine.

My stomach tightened, warmth spreading through my core like it did in the restaurant and again when he carried me up.

His gaze drifted down to where we touched, his brow scrunching as if he could feel the way my body reacted to him. I scooted back, breaking the connection, and he blinked twice, giving his head a tiny shake.

He cleared his throat. "The amulet is the answer to everything. We must find it."

I let out a dry laugh. "We were planning to scry for it this morning. We'd already have it if you hadn't snuck out to roam the streets and nearly gotten us shot."

"Scry for it now."

I rubbed my temples. "We can't."

"Why not?"

"Because scrying takes a lot of vim. Vim is part of a witch's life force. Body, mind, and soul have to work together to replenish it, and even if I had enough in me to go into the trance it requires, I wouldn't be able to come out. My body is injured, my mind is reeling, and my soul is so goddess damned tired I feel like curling into a ball to hibernate."

His head jerked back as if I'd slapped him. "I am to blame for this?"

"Well, yeah." I dropped my arms to my sides. "Not entirely, but having you here isn't making it any easier, and speaking of my mind…" I looked at my sister. "What did you do to me out there? That guy wouldn't have pulled the trigger if I'd kicked his ass, but all I wanted to do was keep the peace. I went from Jason Statham to Mother Theresa in half a second. You promised you'd never mess with my mind."

"We didn't do anything." She looked at Chaos for confirmation, and he shook his head before giving Mayhem a pointed look.

"It was me." He waved a hand dismissively. "I intended to wind you up so I could watch you fight without remorse. Had I known it would have the opposite effect, I would have kept my power to myself."

My mouth hung open, so I snapped it shut. "So you could watch me fight without remorse? I'd have killed them."

"They intended to kill you."

I took a deep breath, holding it for a count of five before releasing it. It was pointless to argue with a demon. He didn't even have a moral compass, much less one that pointed in the right direction. Chaos knew how to behave in this world, because Ash had taught him. He learned because he loved her.

This guy...?

Even if I had the patience to teach him right from wrong, you couldn't pay me enough to try. He was unteachable.

"Now do you believe it's fate?" Ash asked. "Chaos's power has the opposite effect on me too. Some things are meant to be."

Mayhem's face blanked again, but my eyebrows shot toward my hairline. "Are you implying that he and I..." I laughed incredulously. "I'll admit the goddess or *someone* nudged us in the right direction to find these guys. Was it all meant to happen exactly the way it happened? Doubtful."

Ash lifted a finger. "But—"

"But..." I mirrored her pose. "To imply that the universe is now a matchmaker is ludicrous. You and Chaos fell in love. Good for you. But don't you think, if the universe or fate or whatever wanted you to be together, they would have given you a way to *stay* together?"

She straightened, lifting her chin. "Who are we to question fate?"

"Who are we, indeed?" I cast a glance to Mayhem, who looked indifferent AF. He wasn't going to back me up, not that I expected him to.

I stood, testing my weight. When I didn't wobble, I picked up my boot and headed for my room.

"Where are you going?" Ash asked, following me into the hall.

"To shower and change. Miles has an early date with Wendy, and we need to be there to listen." I kicked off my other boot and opened my underwear drawer. The shard of amulet glinted in the overhead light, reminding me how much easier this would be if we didn't have to babysit an unruly demon.

Ash leaned against the dresser, crossing her arms. "Do you seriously not see the way he looks at you?"

"Like he's trying to decide which way he wants to kill me? All the time." I knocked on the drawer her butt was against, and she pushed off, crossing the room to sit on the bed. I yanked it open to find one lonely pair of fireproof pants. "I know it's mean of me to say, but I miss Patrice for the laundry and grocery shopping she did for us. Think we can convince Miles...?"

"Ember, listen to me."

"I will when you speak rationally." I slammed the drawer shut.

"Why is believing in fate so hard for you?"

I tightened my grip on my last pair of pants. "Believing in fate isn't hard. I *truly* believe we were meant to find these guys so we can end the curse. And their magic having the opposite effect on us makes sense. It's karma. They cursed our bloodline, so they can't scramble our brains to bring the curse to fruition themselves."

I grabbed a shirt from the closet. "But Mayhem is not my meant-to-be. I don't believe that person exists for me, but if he does, it is certainly not that arrogant, self-centered brute who doesn't give a flying eff about anyone but himself."

She raised her brows. "He's enamored of you."

I scoffed. "How can you tell? Is it the constant needling, the way he doesn't lift a finger to help me fight, or the fact he lifted me from the ground *by my throat* and threatened to snap my neck?"

She gasped. "He didn't."

"He most certainly did. The only reason he put me down was because I dug a blade two inches into his chest."

"Why didn't you tell me?" She stood and paced toward me. "That's so scary."

"Not really." I shrugged and headed for the bathroom, dropping my clean clothes on the counter before peeling off my socks.

Ash leaned in the doorway. "You don't have to be a badass all the time. It's okay to be scared."

"I wasn't." I unzipped what was left of my pants and fumbled my way out of them.

Ash smiled smugly. "You knew he wouldn't do it."

"No, I didn't."

"Yes, you did."

I took off my shirt and dropped it in the hamper before turning on the tap. "We were at a draw."

She lifted herself onto the counter and swung her legs. "Somewhere, deep inside, you knew he wouldn't kill you. It's not rational because he gave you every indication that he would, but your soul knew he wouldn't."

I rolled my eyes and stepped into the shower, closing the curtain before taking off my bra and undies and tossing them into the hamper. What could I say to that?

"You know I'm right," she sang.

"No, I don't." The hot water felt fabulous beating down on my tired muscles, and the peppermint in my shampoo helped to wake up my mind. Tired and weary didn't begin to describe my level of fatigue.

"And for some goddess only knows reason, even through all the bickering, he's growing on you," Ash said.

"Like a fungus." I stretched my neck beneath the stream, willing the knots in my muscles to release.

"Your body reacts when he touches you."

"Whose wouldn't? He's smoking hot, and you've seen what he's packing." I shut off the water and reached out for a towel.

She handed me one. "You've seen Chaos, too. Does your body react like that when he touches you?"

No. No, it did not. "Chaos is your lover boy, not mine."

"You didn't answer the question."

And I didn't intend to, so I dried off and wrapped the towel around my chest. "Hey, will you text Shade and see how many shadow spells he's bottled? If he's got enough vim, maybe he and Miles can come over and scry for the amulet before the fake date." Because this entire ordeal could not be over quickly enough.

"Done."

As I pulled back the curtain, her phone rang, "Asshole Alert" lighting up the screen.

"Guess I need to change that." She laughed and answered on speaker. "Hey. Em's with me."

"This is Miles." His hushed voice raised the hairs on the back of my neck and made my stomach dip.

"What's wrong? Where's Shade?" I pulled on my undies and shoved my legs into my pants.

"Hold on." A door squeaked on its hinges before clicking shut. I finished getting dressed to the sound of carpet-muffled footsteps.

"He's at my place. He'll be okay, but he didn't get the chance to bottle anything."

I waited a beat. Two. Three. When he didn't continue, I grabbed the phone and brought it to my mouth. "What *happened*?"

"We ran into a soldier. Literally."

Ash gasped, touching her fingertips to her lips, and I jerked my head toward the front of the house.

"Did it bite him?" She followed me to the living room, and I turned up the volume before setting the phone on the coffee table.

"No, thank Hecate," he said. "We caught it off guard, but it was fast. It grabbed me, which let Shade know where it was, even though it was invisible, and he..." Miles drew in a breath, and we all leaned toward the phone. "He sucked the light...the life...out of it. I'd never seen him do it to a sentient being before, but the way it shrieked... It has to be the most painful way to die."

Ash nodded. "It's not pleasant, but getting all the liquid sucked out through your pores might be worse. How's Shade?"

"Sleeping. He said it drains him almost as much as it does his target."

"Because he doesn't practice," Mayhem said. "With the amulet's help, he could be an asset."

"He already is an asset," I said. "He doesn't practice because light witches don't kill people."

Mayhem crossed his arms. "You're Veil Keepers. You kill."

"Vampire ghouls and the occasional gnome or mosquito fae." I matched his posture. "He's never had the need to use that kind of power against a beastie."

"Now he does."

"Anyway…" Miles cleared his throat. "Patrice is coming over to sit with him while I meet with Wendy. From the looks of him, he'll be asleep all night."

"Good. I'm glad she's still willing to help," I said.

"She might not agree with our methods, but she'll do what she can for the good of the coven, just like the rest of us." A faint knocking sounded through the phone. "Oh, she's here."

"What time should we pick you up?" I grabbed my own phone off the counter to check the clock.

"I'll drive myself. I don't want her to be suspicious if she sees me getting out of the coven van. I'm meeting her at six at Pennino's."

"Good plan. We'll be there early and stay out of sight."

"See you then."

Ash ended the call and returned the phone to her pocket. "It would be convenient if Shade could work that kind of magic without completely draining his vim."

"That small piece of the amulet could be enough to help him master it in a short time," Mayhem said. Fabulous. Demon number two never bothered to back me up, but he had no problem agreeing with Ash.

"There's one way to find out." She lifted her hands palms up, and I stared at her with wide eyes. First the coughing when we smudged the room, and now she was willing to experiment on a coven member with magic forged in Hell?

Holy Hecate, we needed to get our butts in gear.

I pointed at Ash. "No." Then at Mayhem. "No. Absolutely no one is messing with the shard. It's broken. It could kill him."

Ash blinked as if finally coming to her senses. "You're right. I don't know why I suggested that."

I looked at Chaos, whose grim expression said we both knew why.

CHAPTER 20
MAYHEM

Had fate finally dealt me a winning hand? I sat in the passenger seat of Ember's van, stealing glances at the enchantress driving us to Boston. Her gaze remained locked on the road, her brow lowered in concentration, and I wondered what thoughts raced inside her mind.

The moment Ash had connected the dots, explaining the reason Ember reacted to my magic the way she did, all the pieces to the puzzle of my existence clicked into place. The tether, which had attempted to connect us previously, solidified, and the flitting of moth wings in my stomach stilled, my chest tightening with resolve.

Ember would be mine.

I had paid my penance. Four centuries in the dark prison in exchange for a warrior princess bride.

It was true fate led me to her. That, I felt in my bones. But the universe knew me too well and presented me with a challenge to overcome. I would tire easily of a damsel falling at my feet, so fate offered me a woman with a fiery heart and a stubborn mind.

She had laughed at the idea that she should belong to me, dismissing any notion that fate had chosen me to be her consort. Winning her heart and mastering her soul would be the greatest challenge I had ever overcome.

Instinct told me to claim what was rightfully mine. When we returned home, I could take the amulet and the woman and return to Hell, where I could spend eternity with her. But she wouldn't come willingly.

She would fight me every step of the way, and while I would enjoy every minute of the fray, I wanted her heart along with her body. No, I would not take her forcefully. I would convince her she and I were meant to be. It was written in the stars four hundred years ago. Perhaps longer.

"We're here." Ember's voice drew me from my thoughts, and she turned toward me. "This is a reconnaissance mission. You are not, under any circumstances, to use your mind magic on anyone. Got it?"

"If your life is threatened..."

"You still don't do it. I can take care of myself." She cocked her head, her pointed look making heat pool in my groin.

She could take care of herself. She had proven that many times since she summoned me, but she also allowed others to care for her when she was in need.

She would learn to need me.

Ember put on a jacket over her shoulder holster. She hid a dagger and three knives beneath her clothing, and she offered another to Ash, who slipped it into her bag.

"If we're only here to gather information, why do you go in armed?" I unbuckled my seatbelt.

"It's Veil Keeper 101. Always be prepared for a fight." She opened her door, and the overhead light illuminated the hard set of her jaw before she exited the vehicle.

I fought the smile tugging at my lips and slid out of my seat, closing the door behind me. "You and Ash are the ruling bloodline of Salem. Will Wendy not recognize you?"

"She would for sure." Ember flipped up her jacket collar, crossing her arms against the stinging autumn wind. "But she'll never see us."

The strange urge to wrap my arms around her and shield her from the cold overtook me. I wasn't keen on having a knife jabbed into my side, so I didn't dare. But the fact she would do it only added to her appeal.

"How will we hear their conversation if we're out of sight?" I asked.

"With technology. Let's grab a table, and I'll explain." She led us to the restaurant, and a young man wearing black pants with a stark white button-up opened the door to greet us.

We entered the restaurant's foyer and found another young man in the same clothing standing behind a podium., his face a mask of boredom and contempt. "What name is the reservation under?"

"We don't have one," Ember replied. "We'll take a table in the back."

"This establishment is reservation only." His judging gaze raked over her form. "And we have a dress code. Yoga pants are not allowed."

Her hands curled into fists. "I don't do yoga. Can we sit at the bar?"

"Not unless you have a reservation."

Her jaw ticked. "It's five o'clock. Most people don't go out for dinner before seven, and you've got dozens of empty tables."

He rolled his eyes. "I can't seat you without a reservation."

"Can I *make* a reservation then?"

His mouth tightened, and he blinked at her twice before lowering his gaze to a tablet screen. "We're booked tonight, but I can get you in next Tuesday."

She stiffened, and I smiled, imagining her wishing she could jab her dagger into the man's neck.

Chaos stepped forward, holding Ash's hand. "The table in the back by the kitchen is free. You'll seat us there."

Our indignant host snapped his gaze to my brother, confusion contorting his features for half a second before they smoothed. "No one ever reserves the table in the back by the kitchen. I'll seat you there. This way."

Interesting...

He picked up a stack of menus and strode into the seating area. I followed silently, taking in our surroundings. A massive crystal chandelier hung in the center of the room, and widely spaced tables covered in white linen held etched glass goblets and gold chargers. Savory scents of garlic and thyme filled the air, and a server passed by carrying a plate covered with a silver dome.

The host waited as we took our seats and then placed a white napkin on each of our laps. He opened the menus one by one, handing them first to the women and then to us. "Your server will be with you shortly. *Bon appetite.*"

Ember shook her head, and I could practically see the thoughts racing through her mind. "I want to berate the two of you, but I know that pompous bitch wouldn't have seated us otherwise."

Ash shrugged. "Sometimes a little gray is necessary."

I narrowed my eyes at my brother. "That didn't look like your normal magic. What did you do?"

"Ash's power counters mine. She can send it to me through the mark she bears, giving me the ability to control minds rather than scatter them."

"And they promised not to do it unless it's absolutely necessary." Ember's shoulders slumped. "Which it was in this case."

Interesting indeed. I wondered how Ember's power might counter mine. If it meant I could guide people to peaceful resolutions, I'd rather not try.

Our server arrived to fill our goblets with water, and Ember ordered a bottle of wine. "We're going to be here a while, but don't worry. We tip well."

"It's fine. This table is rarely sat, so I'm happy to serve you." The woman smiled warmly. "The manager thought it would be a good idea to have a secluded spot for any celebrities who might want to dine in peace." She tugged on a curtain, isolating us from the rest of the dining room. "But he put it right by the kitchen. Guests get annoyed with all the foot traffic, so the idea flopped. I'll be right back with your wine."

"It couldn't be more perfect for us." Ember laid her phone on the table as the server walked away. "Miles will be wearing an earpiece. When he gets here, he's going to call. He'll leave his phone face down on the table so we can hear everything they say."

"Impressive." I nodded my appreciation.

She shrugged. "Sometimes I have good ideas."

She didn't give herself enough credit. Ember was a natural leader. She preferred being in the heat of battle, as did I, but she commanded her small army of Veil Keepers with the skill of a general.

She looked at the menu, and her eyes widened as she let out a low whistle. "They're proud of their food, aren't they? I'm surprised Miles decided to bring her here."

"He probably let her choose," Ash said. "He owes it to her for leading her on."

"These prices are nearly triple those of our lunch restaurant," I said. "I assume you have some form of income to afford it?"

"Ember makes bank at Spellbound Axe in tips alone." Ash sipped her water.

"Not anymore." Ember sighed. "I got fired."

"Damn." Ash grimaced at the menu. "I'll just get a small salad."

"You could use your mind trick to convince our server the food is complimentary." I was surprised they didn't do it all the time.

"Absolutely not." Ember glared at me, making my pulse quicken. "Our world could end in a matter of days, and my credit card is paid off. Order whatever you want. I'll worry about the cost if we make it through."

Our server delivered the meal in courses, with

baked cheese, a salad, and a small bowl of soup coming before the main meal. I didn't dare order the same entrée as Ember, though her steak *foie gras* sounded delicious. My meal consisted of roasted chicken with rosemary potatoes that melted on my tongue. I could get used to the delicacies of this realm.

Ember's phone buzzed on the table, Miles creating the connection for our investigation. A minute or two passed with nothing but muffled sounds before the *clunk* indicated he had set the phone down to begin the interrogation.

I pulled the curtain back slightly, giving myself a view of the pair. Miles wore a brown sports coat—I'd learned the names of modern attire through the television—and Wendy wore a black dress that sparkled in the chandelier light. She had dull brown hair, pulled back in a clip with a lock hanging loose across her forehead.

"I was wondering if you'd ever make good on your promise," Wendy said. We could hear their words clearly through Ember's phone.

"Yeah, sorry about that. With all the rifts forming, I've been busy. Are they bad in Boston too?" Miles got straight to the point. Good man.

"Obviously. Being this close to Salem, we get the aftershock of everything your coven does. How'd you do with the spells from our library? I hope the money one worked so you can pay for the lobster I'm about to order." She lifted her napkin from her lap and wiped her nose, sticking the corner of the cloth into her nostril.

I cringed. "This is the type of woman Miles finds attractive?"

"Good goddess, no." Ember laughed. "He used her to get into the Boston coven library."

Miles cleared his throat, reminding us of his earpiece. He could hear our conversation as well as we heard his.

"Sorry." Ember pressed the mute button, her finger hesitating over the device before she pressed it again. "Steer her back to the rifts and the fae." She muted the call.

Our server cleared our plates and returned with four dishes of *crème brûlée*. As she set them on the table, we heard Miles and Wendy ordering their meals.

"He's our friend," Ash said quickly. "He knows we're listening."

"We're giving him pointers on his date," Ember added.

The server refilled our water goblets. "That's none of my business. I'll give you some privacy." She smiled and walked away.

"So the rifts..." Miles said. "What do you know about them?"

She narrowed her eyes. "That they're happening

more and more, and they're only going to get worse when Halloween rolls around. Why?"

"Just curious." He took a giant gulp of water. "Those fae, though, right? The lesser ones are annoying, but the big guys... Man, they're hard to kill."

Her brow slammed down. "How big? What do they look like?"

"Like giant, venomous bugs with impenetrable exoskeletons."

Her brows crept toward her hairline as she straightened her spine. "You've fought them?"

"My coven has killed three. We found a massive rift just north of Salem. Four or five more probably got through."

Her complexion paled. "Are your fire witches burning them?"

He shook his head. "They're fireproof."

She laid her hands on the table, leaning forward. "How do you kill them?"

They paused their conversation as their food arrived. When their server left, Miles spoke, "You've got them here too, don't you? The serial killer they're talking about on the news? It's the fae."

She swallowed hard, though she had no food in her mouth. "How do you know?"

"They eat human livers so they can survive in this realm. We've done some research, and we think there's going to be an invasion. You might want to warn your coven since they're killing in your territory too."

She picked up a glass of wine and drained the contents in three gulps before wiping her mouth with the back of her hand. "Can you keep a secret?"

Miles leaned toward her. "I won't tell a soul."

She shifted her gaze from left to right before resting a hand on the table. "They're here because of us. Well, because of Adrian, our High Priest. He called them here."

Ember locked eyes with Ash, her expression one of alarm.

"What do you mean?" Miles asked. "They're coming through the rifts. The lesser fae have come through for years."

"The big guys...?" Her hand trembled as she picked up her spoon and scooped the soup. The liquid fell from the utensil before it reached her mouth. "They can make themselves invisible, right?"

Miles nodded.

"It's the same ones then." She blew out a hard breath. "We have several volumes of a fae encyclopedia in our library, and Adrian has been obsessed with reading them. With the veil as thin as it is now, he got this delusional idea that, if he could convince this half-blooded prince to invade, they could join forces and basically take over the world."

Miles tilted his head. "Your High Priest thinks he can achieve world domination with *the fae*?"

"I told you he was delusional." She dipped a piece of bread into her soup and shoved it into her mouth. "It's why I joined Chrys's coup."

Ember unmuted the phone. "Get her to elaborate."

"Obviously," Miles said, quickly straightening at his faux pas. "I mean, that's the obvious thing to do when your leader wants to upset the balance of the realms."

"Right? I tried to tell people that, but they didn't want to listen." She waved a hand dismissively. "If Chrys hadn't gone nutso and tore our library apart, we might not be in this situation. She killed one of your members too. The woman was certifiably batshit."

"Poor Miles." Ash scrunched her face. "The person she killed was Miles's girlfriend."

Anger sparked in my chest. Miles was a loyal witch who obeyed orders without protest. Any coven would be lucky to have members like him. "You should have let me burn through her to avenge his lover's death."

"Shh." Ember pressed a finger to her lips. "Listen."

"We're still reeling from that," Miles said. "How did she recruit? What was her purpose in staging the coup?"

"She was secretive about it all. She'd hang around Boston, catching us when we were alone and feeding us BS about how powerful she was, and that once she summoned some demon prince, she'd have the power to overthrow both Boston and Salem." Her hands steadied, and she poured herself another glass of wine, leaving Miles's glass empty.

"When we told her about what Adrian had done, she promised to stop it from happening. Then she went nuts and got herself killed. I figured we'd be banished, but Adrian forgave us all."

I leaned back in my chair. "He probably planned to feed them to the fae."

"Indeed," Chaos agreed.

"How did Adrian contact the fae?" Miles added more wine to Wendy's glass. I appreciated his interrogation technique. Loose lips spilled more secrets.

"He attached a letter to a lesser fae and sent it through a rift like a carrier pigeon. They went back and forth for a week or so before the scouts arrived. Now that the soldiers are here, though..." She took another drink.

"They're like mindless killing machines." She scoffed. "There's no alliance. Adrian invited the monsters into our realm, and they've already turned against him. I don't think the fae ever planned to work with us."

She swayed in her chair, her words beginning to slur. "You should talk to your High Priestess. Maybe our covens can form an alliance to kick the fae to the curb."

"That's not a bad idea," Miles said.

"Don't tell her about all this though. I'm not even supposed to know the details. People talk in front of me because no one takes me seriously. But we haven't killed a single one. You have, so Adrian will listen to you."

Miles patted her hand on the table. "I'll see what I can do."

CHAPTER 21

MAYHEM

We waited in the restaurant until Miles and Wendy left before returning home. Now, Ember paced in her usual spot in front of the television.

"An alliance with Boston. I can't decide if that's a good idea or a bad one." She unhooked her shoulder holster and laid it on the counter next to her sword. "What do you think?"

I thought she should continue removing the articles she wore, beginning with her shirt. Sadly she didn't ask me.

"Let's think about the pros and cons." Ash sat on the sofa next to Chaos, drumming her fingers on her knees. "We could use the manpower, for sure. Especially if an entire army gets through."

"True, true." Ember clasped her hands behind her

back as she walked. "But keeping our involvement in how this all started a secret has been hard enough with our own coven. And BSM is a dark coven. We can't trust any of them."

I sat in a chair, watching her pace and think. Her mind was as brilliant as her body was beautiful, and though I normally enjoyed discussing battle plans, all I could think about was how to convince her she and I were fated.

"We don't even know if what Wendy said was true." Ash tapped a finger to her lips. "She could have been baiting us."

"Doubtful," Ember said. "Drunk people don't lie."

"I don't get the impression Wendy is of a mind to spin such an elaborate tale," Chaos said. "Or to remember all the details if she were tasked with delivering it."

"No, she's definitely not." Ember stopped and rested her hands on her hips. "What's our next step?"

"What does your gut tell you?" Ash asked.

Ember paused, casting her gaze upward for a moment. "Stay on course. Knowing why the fae are invading doesn't change the fact that they are. It doesn't change anything."

"Right." Ash nodded.

"We chill tonight, scry in the morning, and then we go from there." She gave me a pointed look. "That means *you* have to stay inside and not cause any trouble."

"Perhaps I should sleep in your room so you can keep an eye on me."

"Maybe I should chain you to the bed, so I know you can't move." Her eyes widened as she realized her words conveyed a different meaning. Rather than backtracking on her statement, she crossed her arms and arched a brow.

I couldn't stop the growl from rumbling in my chest.

"Ahem." Ash eyed Ember and tilted her head toward me.

Ember held up a hand. "Don't start."

"I would like to hear what your sister has to say." I rested my elbows on my knees. "We are supposed to be 'chilling' tonight, so let's have a conversation about something other than the direness of our situation."

"Okay." She raised both hands and let them fall at her sides. "Ash insists that just because your mind magic had the opposite effect on me like his does to her, it means you and I are soulmates. Tell her how ridiculous that is."

It wasn't ridiculous in the slightest. I pressed the tips of my fingers together, an idea forming in my mind. "How does Chaos's power affect you?"

She crossed her arms. "He's never tried."

I nodded, the corners of my mouth tugging

upward. "I propose a way to lay the ridiculousness—or truth—of Ash's hypothesis to rest."

"I'm listening."

I rose to my feet. "Allow me to hold Ash's mind for a moment. Just long enough for her to feel the effect and act accordingly. Once we have our answer, I'll release her and never use my power on her again."

Ember drummed her fingers against her biceps. "No way. Neither one of you is going to mess with our minds."

Ash's face held a thoughtful expression before she raised her brows at my brother. "I'm game if you trust him. At the very least, it'll put Ember's mind at ease."

"Or it will prove we are, in fact, soul mates."

She rolled her eyes. "It won't prove that, but okay. Fifty bucks says you can't make Ash violent. Her magic will counter yours."

"I could never take money from someone who just lost her job. How about this instead?" I leaned against the counter, crossing my legs at the ankles. "If Ash's magic counters mine, I will become your obedient servant. If I can make her violent, you agree to share your bed with me...for sleeping purposes only...unless you wish to do more."

She raised her chin, her eyes calculating. "Sleeping only? You won't touch me?"

"Not until you want me to." I offered my hand to shake.

"It doesn't matter. You're going to lose, anyway." She placed her palm in mine.

Ash chuckled. "I never thought I'd see the day when Ember made a deal with a demon."

"Indeed," Chaos said.

"Whatever." She tugged from my grasp. "Let's get this over with."

Ash stood and padded across the room, dragging Chaos behind her. "I'm going to stand over here just in case. I doubt I'm strong enough to hurt a demon if I do get violent, so I'll stay close to him."

"You swear you'll release her the second she feels the magic?" Ember moved next to me.

"You have my word."

She blew out a hard breath, her expression skeptical.

"I'll be fine," Ash said. "I want to know how he'll affect me."

"And if he doesn't release her, I will make him." Chaos flashed a cold, hard stare in my direction, the silent threat imminent, though I had no intention of holding Ash any longer than necessary.

She would turn violent, and while I would enjoy watching her try to beat my brother, my purpose for this experiment was singular.

To convince Ember she should be mine.

I continued leaning, making my posture as casual as possible to keep the women calm. At Chaos's nod, I called on my magic, sending a trickle toward Ash. She looked back at me, either not feeling the effect or calming, like Ember had done. It could not be the latter. I refused to let it be.

I gathered my power, letting it build in my being, growing stronger with each breath I took. On a hard exhale, I pushed the brunt of it out, seizing Ash's mind. Her eyes widened, and she blinked rapidly, but still she did not move.

"See?" Ember said. "No violence."

Ash heaved a breath. She grunted. And then she screamed.

She whirled toward Chaos, her fist striking his stomach. When he didn't flinch, she growled.

"No violence, eh?" I chuckled and drew my magic back, but a thread of it stuck, hung up on some part of her psyche like a fishhook in seaweed. She drew her arm back and punched again.

"Let her go." Ember clutched my shoulder and shook me.

"I'm trying." My pulse raced, my head aching with the exertion. I pulled and pulled, but the thread remained.

Chaos grabbed Ash from behind, pinning her arms to her sides as she kicked and wailed. "Release her!" he boomed.

"I can't." I moved closer, desperately trying to

sever the tie between her mind and mine. "Something is wrong. It's stuck. It's…"

The sigil on her arm pulsed bright red. "It's your mark. It's holding my magic."

"Turn it off." Ember snarled. "You're hurting her."

"If I could, I would." I turned toward her, and the anger burning in her eyes morphed into hatred.

Lucifer help me. What had I done?

"I'm trying. I don't want to hurt her." My mind scrambled for a solution, but before my thoughts caught up with what was happening, Ember lunged for her sword. The rest of the events unfolded in slow motion.

Screaming like a scorned Valkyrie, she spun, raising the blade above her head and hurling it downward at an angle, slicing into my neck. My head hit the ground, my eyes wide with shock as Ash heaved a breath, finally free of my hold.

Ember's blade pierced my chest, searing silver penetrating through my heart, the force of her jab sending it out through my back until the hilt met my flesh. Her hand in my hair, lifting me from the floor, was the last thing I felt, Ash's breathy voice the final thing I heard before the dark prison yanked me across the veil…

"Oh my goddess, Ember. What have you done?"

ALSO BY CARRIE PULKINEN

Fire Witches of Salem Series

Chaos and Ash

Commanding Chaos

Claiming Chaos

Mayhem and Ember

Mending Mayhem

Mastering Mayhem

New Orleans Nocturnes Series

License to Bite

Shift Happens

Life's a Witch

Santa Got Run Over by a Vampire

Finders Reapers

Swipe Right to Bite

Batshift Crazy

Collection One: Books 1-3

Collection Two: Books 4 - 7

Crescent City Wolf Pack Series

Werewolves Only

Beneath a Blue Moon

Bound by Blood

A Deal with Death

A Song to Remember

Shifting Fate

Collection One: Books 1-3

Collection Two: Books 4-6

Haunted Ever After Series

Love at First Haunt

Second Chance Spirit

Third Time's a Ghost

Love and Ghosts

Love and Omens

Love and Curses

Collection One: Books 1 - 3

Collection Two: Books 4 - 6

Stand Alone Books

Flipping the Bird

Sign Steal Deliver

Azrael

Lilith

The Rest of Forever

Soul Catchers

Bewitching the Vampire

About the Author

Carrie Pulkinen is a paranormal romance author who has always been fascinated with things that go bump in the night. Of course, when you grow up next door to a cemetery, the dead (and the undead) are hard to ignore. Pair that with her passion for writing and her love of a good happily-ever-after, and becoming a paranormal romance author seems like the only logical career choice.

Before she decided to turn her love of the written word into a career, Carrie spent the first part of her professional life as a high school journalism and yearbook teacher. She loves good chocolate and bad puns, and in her free time, she likes to read, drink wine, and travel with her family.

Connect with Carrie online:
CarriePulkinen.com